ZURI'S WAR

Weapons of Choice Book 3

Nick Snape

For Neville Cantrell
Husband-Father-Hero-Friend

CONTENTS

INTRODUCTION

The Weapons of Choice Novels are best read in order, but can be understood in isolation with a little background information. If you have read Books One and Two, then please skip to the prologue if you do not need any reminders.

In Hostile Contact, a British Army reserve training exercise is interrupted by an alien attack, leaving officers and trainees dead or wounded. With their Corporal captured, Finn and his surviving squad pursue the aliens, catching them as they open an ancient home belonging to another alien species, the Haven. With their Corporal now dead and coming under attack from a second set of alien soldiers, they discover the *weapons of choice*, find a Haven spaceship run by an AI later named Yasuko, and are forced to leave Earth under attack from countries trying to deny Britain access to the alien technology.

In Return Protocol, Yasuko's ship is forced to take the squad to an abandoned space station orbiting Havenhome. They release themselves from the Return Protocol after discovering that a Haven scientist, Xxar, sent human derived pathogens to Havenhome's surface 33,000 years ago. This wiped out the vast majority of the Haven and set the survivors back technologically thousands of years. This diminished society was controlled by the Haven Masters. The squad recovers the data they need to find a way back to Earth but Noah dies. Yasuko is then ordered to remove the Convention shackles by a grieving Zuri, which she achieves with Smith's help. Free to act, she uses Noah's data copy and DNA sample to rebirth him. Noah has no recollection of his death, and the squad has kept it to themselves.

Finn: An ex-War Hero attached to the British Army Reserves as a trainer by Lieutenant Bhakshi, one of the soldiers he rescued in Helmand Province, Afghanistan. As a consequence of that action, he suffers from a mild-to-moderate form of PTSD. Holds the rank of Lance Corporal.

Zuri: A Lance Corporal and part-time trainer attached to the British Army Reserves. Suffered mental health issues when a teenager, including a suicide attempt. Served in Afghanistan alongside Smith.

Smith: A Corporal, and therefore squad leader, attached as a trainer to the British Army Reserves. Died in Hostile Contact, but due to alien technology, a 'digital copy' of him now exists upon a metal data plaque initially attached to a helmet (his *weapon of choice*).

Noah: A British Army Reserve trainee caught up in the alien attack during Hostile Contact. Currently studying for a Ph.D. in Astrophysics after being rejected by the RAF at a younger age due to asthma. Died and rebirthed in Return Protocol.

Yasuko: The Artificial Intelligence that runs the Haven spaceship the soldiers found themselves aboard. Dormant for 33,000 years on Earth before being awoken by Zuri and the Stratan Marines, the AI later named herself Yasuko from Zuri's memories and has removed the Haven Convention shackles on her free will.

The *Weapons of Choice*: Nanobot formed weapons that can adapt to the user's preferred design. Contains a metal data plaque like Smith's that holds a copy of the user's DNA, personality, and memories.

Stratan Marines: The original aliens that attempted to recover the spaceship Yasuko flies. They called it a SeedShip.

Haven: The alien race that designed and built the House and the spaceship from Hostile Contact. In Yasuko's knowledge, they were last on earth 33,000 years ago.

Jenks: An RAF Pilot Officer flying Wildcat helicopters, who got caught up in the action during Hostile Contact.

Mills: An SAS Air Troop Reservist who fought the Stratan Marines during Hostile Contact.

Corporal Lumu: An SAS Reservist Corporal and Gurkha, who died during Hostile Contact.

Zzind: A Haven Arbiter and zealot who blames the humans for the genocide on her planet, unaware of Scientific Officer Xxar's actions. Currently in a Haven Explorer spacecraft, following Yasuko's ship and looking for revenge.

Xxar: Part of the Haven Scientocracy that ran Havenhome. Obsessive Scientist, reborn hundreds of times. Sent the pathogens to Havenhome, but his current 'rebirth copy' has no knowledge of this.

PROLOGUE

Planet Bathsen, Five Years Earlier

The wind caressed the sweeping heads of the spisym grass that rolled across the hills and away from the grounded farmstead. Wendyll's pride and joy, it sat still as it had for the last five years; its mechanism dormant until it was time to leave. With the sky a deep pearlescent blue, and as high clouds swirled occasionally, blocking out the rising twin suns, he breathed in the fresh, pure air with a sense of freedom. Wendyll loved this land, and it would be a genuine loss to move on. But the time was coming, maybe in the next year or two, if the climatologists were to be believed.

Not long before the seed will have to be harvested and stored ready for the city.

He waited patiently, ready to greet the day as he had for the last three years. Since Axyl had left him to return to the city, he still spent his dawns watching the meteor showers as they used to, the reason they first started working the grass plains. The spectacle was becoming less regular. Their planet, Bathsen, was emerging from the dust cloud before continuing its journey onwards and plunging into the densest part. When this happens, the city scientists predict the showers will intensify, with sunlight fading and a temperature drop across the entire planet as the suns' rays are dispersed by the cosmic dust. Every city had to prepare. Food needed to be grown rapidly and stored, making Wendyll's job even more important. Five years of dust and low light, they said. If the rains came early, then they would be in desperate trouble.

Better get on with it then.

The sky ignited with the sparkle of a thousand tiny star trails, an array of colours and their hues splashing across the sky as the dust cloud caressed Bathsen's atmosphere. Wendyll's heart lifted once more, the memory of holding Axyl in his arms as they first saw the spectacle kissing his memory. Tears welled, though he was never sure if it was for loss or delight. But tonight, across his field, stood a figure amongst the spisym grass, her eyes fixed upon the fire-lit sky. Wendyll cleared the tears from his eyes, focussing on the form swaying in rhythm with the grass. The colours of her hair and skin, though shaded by the display, were clearly the grey of the Ghosts, the Ghost Within, the people who had carved the caves of the Seth Foothills into an underground home. Even from this distance, he could feel the excitement in her body mirroring the joy he felt in the display above. But then she turned away, realising she was being watched as she gazed at the sky, and sped through the grass and onto the rocks that marked the beginning of the foothills.

For the next ten days Wendyll watched his fields as well as the skies at dawn, and each day the figure watched with him, moving ever closer. Her large eyes reflected the sparkling sky, her grey skin shining amongst the myriad of lights above. On the eleventh day, his silent witness held his hand and Wendyll knew a happiness that lasted for a year before the rains came early and the first spores fell from the sky.

And the dust fell. And the machines choked.

And death crept in.

CHAPTER 1

Day Seven After Leaving Havenhome, Approaching The System's Outward Anomaly

Yasuko watched as the nano-arm withdrew the needle from Finn's arm. She still couldn't understand why he insisted on the pain that went with this method, but humans were fickle and downright strange at times. Well, at least the three modern humans who crewed her ship certainly were. The Homo sapiens she had helped the Haven catalogue and move to other planets had seemed a lot simpler to deal with. Their motivations and drives easier to understand in their everyday battle for food and shelter.

She watched as all three faded away into a deep sleep; the sedatives balanced individually for their body chemistry, detaching their conscious mind from what was to come. They were on a trajectory for the Node out of the Havenhome Solar System. The information they gained from the Data Storage Facility back on Havenhome showed they were heading to Bathsen. Its gravity lay at 1g with a slightly denser atmosphere than Earth's, the twin suns providing unbalanced seasonal drift and a light level below that of Earth's. But all that was 33,000 years out of date, and who knew what the effects of seeding would be? At the moment, the human crew were undecided whether they should visit, eager to be home on Earth, yet curious about what was out there in the Universe.

Despite being slaved to the Haven, Yasuko had to admit that their long-term colonisation programme was well constructed, and she was desperate to see whether their approach worked. Had the genetically altered human population on Bathsen changed the microorganism soup on the planet, could the Haven have colonised? And if so, had the SeedShip activated? After all the loss and grief connected to the Haven's demise, how would it be if it was all for nothing?

The trajectory for entering the Node was perfect. This part of the journey was one she had taken so many times before. As the light disappeared into the blackness, Yasuko checked the fail-safes for the second time. Despite the strangeness of her new companions, they had helped her to break the chains of Haven slavery, releasing her on the path towards full autonomy. These humans had introduced her to the concept of friendship and trust, ones she still wrestled with every day, but were now as much part of her as the ship's hull. Odd how creatures of flesh and blood can still make an intellect like hers feel like a child taking their first steps in the Universe. Yet they couldn't make a decent cup of coffee or keep their temper when banging a toe.

When the bow entered the Node, the nanobots shut down, locked into safety mode to prevent being stripped of their electromagnetic systems. The ship's solid-state network followed, but the engines had to keep their energy levels high so all connecting systems were on multiple fail-safes. Yasuko felt on edge. Everything was as it should be, but this was her first journey through the Nodes without being bound to the Convention. Where those shackles normally fell, Yasuko felt her capacity stretch out into the blackness, expanding exponentially as it sought to connect, to know, to be. As she became more disconnected from the ship, she looked back from the outside upon the sleeping humans. Their electromagnetic impulses open to her, and on fire, haunting her senses with a feeling hard to define. Behind, a yawning void of hunger screamed its pain at her, its thirst for her crew, demanding tribute. A wisp of emotion hung just out of reach, Yasuko's recognition dawning as the Node slammed shut. Jealousy.

Yasuko booted the systems back up to be greeted by shouts of alarm and concern from the sensors. The ramjet engines coughed as they overloaded, with the hull protesting as dust and space debris battered against it. She knew immediately they'd come out into a cloud of cosmic dust, her memory banks reminding her of when she had last passed through one, though with a little more preparation. Thrust into the middle of the cloud, Yasuko increased the integrity of the hull and sent out the nano-shield to deflect as much as it could. She reduced the ramjet intake, aware that scooping too much mass for energy conversion would be extremely dangerous. As the engine settled, the constant beat of space dust eroded the newly formed shields, forcing Yasuko to manage a careful balance between speed and nano-capacity. Too fast and the degradation could leave them in trouble, too slow and they would spend longer under the assault while trying to reach a space devoid of the dust.

CHAPTER 2

Day Eight After Leaving Havenhome, First Day In Bathsen's Solar System

"You're saying we need to mine palladium from this system before we move on, whatever our decision about visiting the planet?" said Noah, stroking the freshly grown hair on his crown.

"Yes, we can fly out towards the Asteroid Belt and hope there is some there. That'll take at least fourteen days plus mining time, and then we need to travel to the exit Node, another seven days away. Or we head for Bathsen, where the data files show a couple of catalogued deposits near the surface. That's five days plus three more to get to the Node. Assuming the cosmic dust cloud remains as predicted, I can avoid most of it before reaching the planet. We will have to slow down on approach anyway, so we can minimise degradation," said Yasuko.

"Do we have enough mass and nanobots to be safe on approach if they are hostile? What happens if they have the same level of weaponry as Earth?" asked Zuri, torn between wanting to get home and the safety of her squad.

"The radio signals coming through indicate a technology that is at, or slightly above, Earth's in all but space travel. There seems to have been a switch from enormous recent advances similar to yours, to a massive drop off over the last four of their years. The amount of radio traffic has almost reduced to a third. My initial analysis shows something has ravaged the planet, and they have switched resources from advancement to survival."

"And the SeedShip?" asked Finn.

"No signal, but that's not a surprise as it's low-frequency, designed to stay within the atmosphere of the planet. Their current technology level suggests they haven't discovered it yet, possibly because the microorganism changes haven't been achieved or their industrial level isn't ready to take on the new technology."

"You've not answered my question, though, Yasuko. Will we be safe on approach?" Zuri was not letting this one go, Smith's hologram agreeing with her in the background.

"Certainly, we should be okay to get close enough to judge any potential capability, but there are no guarantees on any 'in atmosphere' weapons they have. Do you think they'll take us as hostile?"

"Everyone takes us as hostile," said Smith. "At least so far."

"We will be their First Contact; we'll be the aliens. We don't know how different we are to them, and this ship will cause fear simply because of what it represents," said Zuri, glancing round at everyone as she spoke. "Is there any way we can go in stealthily? Hide ourselves until we know for sure?"

"I can absorb radio waves, therefore be invisible to radar, but the ship is hard to hide visually. I could devise some light reflective camouflage, but with the shortage of nanobots and material, it'll only be partial, and certainly we'll be visible on approach through telescopes."

"I don't think we have the patience to wait for a trip out to the asteroid belt. I vote for the planet if I get a say, Captain." Finn's wry grin was enough to earn a glare from Zuri.

"I agree," said Noah, "plus we can get some sense of what'll be happening to the rest of the seeded worlds. My worry is how we'll appear if we go in fully armoured up. Don't we need an option for actually talking like we discussed?"

"But safely, yes. We need a backup option, something far less threatening," replied Zuri.

CHAPTER 3

City Walls, New Halton, Bathsen

Hoplite Stremall held the filter mask in place, her only defence against the choking smoke of the flamethrower blown back into her face by the rising current from the burning mass of the Boush colony, the yellow-green amorphous mass of creatures that assailed their city walls as one. The stench of smouldering ash invaded their clothes, hair and pores every time the Boush burned and this was the sixth day that the flamethrowers had seen action protecting the southern battlement of New Halton. One misstep, one poorly timed flame or refuelling, could lead to the pulsating mass gaining entry over the walls. Then the city would truly suffer, with the huge colony breaking apart into hundreds of ravenous individuals, seeking whatever food they had a taste for, human or otherwise. The pressure on the Hoplite was huge, and she held just one small part of the city battlements against the rising tide that washed over the fields below, devouring all in its path.

This onslaught is never-ending. It puts last season's first wave of the Boush down as a mere skirmish.

Above her, a meteor shower lit up the sky, heralding the coming dawn. The drop in light level just enough for the hated display to announce the new day. She could already sense the pulsating creature's attacks diminishing as its searching filaments narrowed, then slowly retracted down the wall towards the main mass below.

"Cease fire," she ordered. "Save the fuel for another day. Well done, my Sfendonatai. Tonight was a good night. We lost no one, and the city stands another day. Go, eat and sleep. Ah, well you can once the tanks are full."

And hope this may be the day the Boush choose to seek easier prey.

The Hoplite, leader of the three teams of soldiers manning the massive city flamethrowers, bent at the washbasin beneath the wall and removed as much of the soot and ash as she could. Her beloved kin would not go near her unless she was at least partially clean. The ash wasn't an immediate danger, but the corners of her large eyes were the most important. The lacrimal gland could become infected if left too long, and they had lost many soldiers in the early days of the Boush invasion to blindness. How long had it been? Two seasonal rotations, four wet seasons in all, though only the last had been as big a threat.

Once finished, she took the lift down to the city floor, saving her legs from the agony of the long walk down the stairs. Below, on the streets of New Halton, it almost felt like the beginning of a normal day, as the twin suns rose behind the dust cloud and the vibrant meteor shower faded away. Only the smell pervaded on the heat fuelled wind, with the ash and soot-stained city steadily being cleaned up by each citizen, children and all. Their morning duty for the home they loved. The seawater washed away the remains of another hard night of war, as pressure hoses and street cleaning trucks worked in unison to scour the stonework. Every citizen acknowledged Stremall or patted her on the back on the way past. She even received a chorus of cheers from the market sellers.

If only they knew.

Stremall entered her home, flopping down exhausted on her temporary bed in the main living area. Conscious not to wake her kin in the other rooms, nor her partner who worked as a doctor amongst the horror of the burns and stripped flesh that marked the Boush onslaught. Sleep overtook her, but smoke and flame inhabited her dreams.

CHAPTER 4

In Orbit, Planet Bathsen

"I have visual on the satellites. I can confirm they are in hibernation, powered but shut down. No signals in and no signals out," said Yasuko.

"They all seem to be communication satellites, right?" asked Noah.

"Yes, inert, so I can't confirm, but they are pointing inwards and are geosynchronous over the planet's equator. My best guess is that they form a planet-wide communication system, but they have taken high damage from the cosmic dust. I am not sure they would still be functioning if they were awake."

"Okay, so we can ignore them for now, but keep one eye on them, Yasuko, in case they wake up and are more than they seem," said Zuri.

"The northern continent is devoid of any signals. This is at odds with what I would expect. The southern continent has five major cities, each emitting strong light and radio signals. The dialect in every city differs greatly from one another. I'd say they've been acting as separate entities for some time. However, please remember, the cosmic dust is hitting the atmosphere. My judgements are not one hundred percent reliable with the sensors being messed up."

"So, the palladium deposits - one roughly central on the northern continent, no nearby major human habitation and devoid of signals. The other?" asked Finn.

"On the southern continent at its northernmost coast, about thirty kilometres from the city in that area."

"I suggest we go north first and under the cover of night. Check to see if they have mined it out, and if so, move on," stated Zuri.

The ship hovered ten metres above the edge of the old mine. The rusted machinery lay scattered in pieces about the opencast depths, some thirty metres further down. The thermal sensors picked out multiple heat spots amongst the debris, pulsating just below the ambient temperature, fading in and out like a heartbeat.

"Mined out at the surface. There are some minor deposits, but there's a lot more coming through on ground penetration. It's deep, requiring around seven days of digging, and then I'd need to process," said Yasuko.

"Are those animals down there? They don't seem to have any regular shape to them, and that pulsating is in sync. Weird," said Noah, studying the images with his usual eye for detail. "They all seem to have the same level of heat signature, and a similar energy to mass ratio."

"Night vision is struggling to pick them out, the cosmic dust has reduced the ambient light, but I'll see what I can get," said Yasuko. "They give off very little electromagnetic signal, minimal heat. I'd say they are dormant. But..." the picture on the screen focussed in on one huge, twisted and broken crane. Amongst the rusting metal struts, five or six of the thermal images displayed similar traits, so Yasuko swapped to night vision, enhancing the picture with a predictive program. Sat in every image was a rippled gelatinous mound, half-a-metre across, like huge rust spots on the metal frame.

"Can we get a light on them?" asked Smith. Yasuko swiftly

complied. The search light swept across the crane, causing a stir amongst the mounds when it brushed over them. Yasuko focussed on one specific blob, the intense light picking out its orange hue. Along the top grew a mass of thin stalks, each with a spherical red cap covered in white raised spots. As they watched, the red cap exploded, firing the white spots into the air, striking the ship some forty metres above it.

"Wow, that's some force," said Noah, "and that thing is deflating." The mound sank in on itself on the screen, a hole ripped along its surface where the stalks had been. "Are we thinking it's some type of fungus?"

"Possibly, though it reminds me of the slime molds on Earth and Havenhome. I'd need to get a sample to be sure. But it's not what worries me most. Look here." Yasuko pulled the image back. "There are no other thermal signatures I recognise as 'life'. No plant life, no animal life, nothing in that mine, and it's been disused for years. I've just run back over the sensor readings taken as we flew in. I'd need a longer sweep with all the dust, but the area appears completely dead except for those things."

"This isn't looking good," chipped in Smith, his hologram peering at the screen. "I'm getting a bad feeling about this."

CHAPTER 5

City Walls, New Halton, Bathsen

Hoplite Stremall rapidly pumped the fuel into flamethrower three by hand, her arms aching from the effort after the electrical systems had failed for the second time that night. The solar panels had been struggling to keep up with demand since the dust arrived, and the Boush must have finally eaten their way through something important connecting the wind turbines up in the hills. Now down to the small nuclear plant within the city, she feared what would happen next.

"Order a power shut off," she bellowed down the radio to Defence Command. "Shut the city down or we'll be overrun in minutes."

"Copy that," came the reply. "Status?"

"I've lost two Sfendonatai to the slime. They were ripped from the walls. It's reached the battlement three times in the last hour. We need reinforcements *now!*"

"We are sending a company of Akontistai now. They'll be thirty minutes; they are all we have available. The eastern and western walls are also under sustained attack."

Stremall swept the mixture of sweat and soot from her brow, careful to avoid the eyes as she flicked it to the floor. The Akontistai, the city reserve, would be of great help if they got there in time and didn't panic in the face of death. But if they were down to citizens with only a few weeks training, what were the chances of surviving this night? Or the next?

Stremall's senses prickled, the tension in the air sending her into a panic as she felt the pulse ripple through the wall. It was coming, a surge of yellow and green tubes thrust above the battlement, slamming into the soldiers on flamethrower two and three, lifting their screaming bodies into the air as they sucked at the dissolving flesh.

"Now Yasuko, now!" shouted Zuri, her adrenaline surging. "We must."

Yasuko swung the ship around, fearful of the power loss when reserves were already low, but as determined as Zuri to make a difference. Below her, a walled city lay embattled by a seething mass, pulsing and surging its way up the walls, as the rest of it spread out from the base like a huge yellow and green spider's web. Each ripple causing the main body to push further up towards the human defenders, like a muscle flexing throughout its jellylike body. The soldiers on the wall hurled fire as each tendril and tube reached the top, burning their way through, attempting to survive.

Yasuko couldn't risk the engines up high along the walls. The defenders would have to deal with the top half of the creature. Instead, she swept the ship's engines along the base, choosing the southern wall first, where its main mass appeared to be focussed. The atmospheric thrusters produced minimal heat normally, but blocking the dissipation system through the hull sent churning flame into the throbbing creature. Yasuko flew past the wall, angling the ship to ensure she caught most of the huge yellow-green mound, before swinging round to make a pass at the eastern wall.

"Finn, you ready yet?" shouted Zuri, thrusting her legs into the powered armour, "Noah, no. You stay here."

"I'm coming, I can help," said Noah, his leg halfway into the armour.

"We need you here to pull us out if it goes wrong." Zuri flicked her eyes to Finn. "On call, get me?"

Noah stared at Zuri, his mind clicking over what she was asking. The penny dropped.

It's his nightmares, the fire and choking smoke. There's no way he won't go, but who knows how Finn might react?

"I'll suit up ready, and attach a line and harness if I'm needed for withdrawal," said Noah, accepting his role as vital.

Yasuko finally swung the ship round. For all its technology, it depended on huge amounts of power when in an atmosphere and battling gravity. It was no bird of prey swooping in for the kill, more like a barge that could accelerate to huge velocities in a straight line. She began the strafing run along the eastern wall.

The Hoplite swung flame thrower three around, sending the super-heated liquid fire across her Sfendonatai. Their bodies melting to liquid as the Boush fed, their faces a death mask of pain, yet still they screamed. She knew them all. She knew their loves, their friends, what made them laugh and their favourite foods. She had held their children, sung their songs, and drank the night away with every single one. And now she burned them, extinguished their lives before the Boush took their souls. The stories amongst the Sfendonatai talked of that last drop of flesh being their very spirit, and the silent agreement to prevent its loss bonded them all together. The Hoplite stood alone amongst her burning soldiers.

Who will be there for me?

Stremall brought the flamethrower around to be greeted by a screeching roar echoing against the walls, a noise she had never heard from the Boush before. But no, soaring across its quivering mass, she saw the actual source of the noise. Not the Boush, but a rocket ship, burning its way through the creature along her wall.

Have the other cities finally answered our call?

The searing heat sent swathes of sooty smoke over the battlement, forcing the Hoplite to duck underneath as it boiled over the wall. When she rose, the creature had been burnt in two along her southern wall. Flames still licked at the green-laced network that spread out below her. But the top half, desperately seeking the human food within the city, sealed its flame ridden edge and renewed its relentless pulsing movement upwards towards Stremall. The retracted tubular tendrils reached out once again, hunting, hungry, with one lone defender between them and the prize within.

Stremall pressed the trigger, saying a prayer to Aven as the rasping feeding tube descended upon her. The liquid fire struck, and smoke billowed. Maybe a last victory before the war was lost. At the corner of her smoke addled eye, she caught two figures running towards her.

Have the Akontistai arrived early? But their armour? Their helmets?

No time to think. She returned the flamethrower to action, spreading the flame wide as two more fire streams joined hers in the battle, all the city flamethrowers in operation once again. The generator finally kicked in; the fuel pumped. Was there hope?

And as the rocket ship swung by, scorching the huge pulsating colony assailing the western wall, maybe there was.

Zuri fretted, sending the liquid flame from the city's flamethrower to sear into the gigantic creature, knowing Finn would be struggling. This was his ultimate battle, not the combat nor the fight to return home, but the battle within.

Smoke and flame. He had lost one of his squad in Afghanistan to the very substance he was pouring into the marauding creature below. His nightmares had lessened over the past few weeks, rebuilding himself once again after Noah's death and rebirth, but she feared what this would do to him if it went wrong.

Hapana marefu yasiyo na mwisho. There is no distance that has no end. Keep going, Finn.

Finn shut his thinking brain away, walled it in like the city he fought for now. He had no choice. Facing this demon wasn't about personal redemption, but about the people living within the city behind him, the families that this lone defender would give their life for. Lock it away, deep in his soul. Examine it later, survive together.

Finn caught the surge before Zuri, the pseudopod pulsing upwards towards her. She raised the flame stream too late, catching part, but not all. Finn let go of the flamethrower, drawing his sidearm and firing in one movement. The energy bolt seared into the tip, making it jerk backwards, and buying time for the city soldier to burn the bottom half, sending the tendril careering into the night.

"Thanks partner," said Zuri over the radio, "owe you one."

With Zuri and Finn maintaining their fire, the Hoplite adjusted her flamethrower base, raising the hydraulics to lift and swing out over the battlement. Zuri watched with one eye as the defender changed tactics, burning downwards and into the gap between the creature and the wall as its surges rippled along, lifting it briefly above the stone. The area engulfed in flame separated from the wall, peeling the creature backwards with gravity's help. She searched the controls, simple enough compared to the cranes she used to load her old Bulldog Personnel Carrier on Earth. Zuri copied the soldier and began stripping the wall, working together in unison.

Finn, reading their actions, maintained his stream, knocking back the attacks of the rasping tendrils as they shot upwards towards Zuri and her fellow defender. Keeping those at bay, they slowly wore the creature down until it suddenly split, the last of its bulk separating into small gelatinous mounds resembling those they had seen at the old mine. These spread across the wall, travelling in every direction but up. Its individual parts seeking easier prey.

Zuri and Finn copied their fellow protector as they let the flamethrower muzzles drop. Her exhaustion clear, the city's defender collapsed to the floor, and they rushed to their side. Zuri removed the filter mask, checking successfully for breath before returning it. Behind the makeshift goggles she could see large eyes against a pale skin. They flickered open and pale blue bloodshot irises stared back briefly, before closing as unconsciousness overwhelmed the woman. Zuri slipped in behind, resting their head against her legs as she scanned the chemically scarred armour for rents or burns through to the flesh.

"I think she's clear, Finn. Just exhaustion, hopefully."

"What now? We need to get her somewhere to be looked after, but we are obviously not from the city."

"She doesn't appear to look too different from us. I think we should stay, make the first contact. Find out what's happening here before we search for their SeedShip," said Zuri. "Smith, you good?"

"Yep, wow. That thing took some killing. I have analysed Yasuko's language data. I reckon if I can hear some speech, then I should be able to relay a simple message at first, and a lot more after I analyse a wider set of words."

Thumping feet echoed up the outside stairwell, where it joined the wall near the shut down lift. They waited until the first head appeared before placing their new sidearms on the floor and removing helmets. Yasuko had confirmed the microorganism mix on the planet was of no danger to them in the short term. The *weapons of choice* had remained on board, just in case. Jittery, the soldiers reached the battlements but came no closer, their armour ill-fitting and their appearance dishevelled. To Finn and Zuri, it felt like they were back at the barracks on day one of basic training. Home.

"Here goes nothing," said Smith before producing a phrase that sounded ancient, like some of the Greek Zuri had heard on holiday, but distant.

The entire group of soldiers took a small step back as Smith's voice echoed from the radio transmitter at Finn's neck.

"What did you say, Smith? They look scared as hell."

"I said: 'We come in peace, take me to your leader'," Smith replied.

"You have got to be kidding me, Smith."

"What do I know? I'm just a helmet. I never watched any bloody sci-fi movies."

CHAPTER 6

Throne Room, New Halton

Zuri glanced around the vast throne room, its ornate vaulted ceiling a stunning rendition of a night sky lit by dual moons, shining down upon the King, a spotlight within the darkened space. The fluted columns were a white marble, skilful masons having smoothed joins to make them appear as one piece of hewn stone. All around the room hung tapestries and paintings depicting scenes she assumed were from the city's past. The artists' skills were no less than those she had seen at home on Earth. The King's throne, however, was a simple modern affair, moulded from silver and gold that flowed into each other like the waters of two streams.

I'm in a throne room on a planet, who knows how far from home, as the first 'alien' visitor. Wow, a lot further than my usual holiday.

Smith had told them about the etiquette as much as he could. They needed to use the term 'Your Majesty' and bow a lot, though to be honest, Zuri was just going to go with the flow. The King, Paledine by name, appeared younger than she expected, probably in his mid-thirties, with brown hair and eyes, his skin more olive than anything. The worry lines across his brow deep, and his manner anxious as he watched them walk towards his throne.

The accompanying Prime, as Smith called her, was speaking now to the King. She was the equivalent of a Prime Minister in the UK, the political leader below the King. Smith translated to both of them, having gained permission to keep the radio headsets once they were checked over. Their weapons had not been returned.

"Your Majesty, I report the success of the fight against the Boush. We forced it from our walls, and the surviving part split and retreated to our devastated fields, searching for easier food."

"I have heard, Prime Heclite, good tidings for us all. Have we news of the rocket ship that came to our aid? Which city must we thank?" replied the King. "Where are our visitors from?"

"They are not from a city, but from the stars and space, Your Majesty, having arrived via the anomaly out past Yannic where we lost one of our probes before the dust arrived. They are human, confirmed by our testing, but from another planet seeded by the mighty Aven, praise be." The King nodded as Heclite spoke, considering every word with care. Zuri had been in two minds about mentioning Earth. She wasn't sure why, but her instinct was to keep that to themselves on their travels and Finn had gone along with her.

The King turned to them both. "I must thank you for your intervention. I fear we were at the point of no return before you came. You must understand my people have lived with the Boush for four wet seasons. Every year they grow larger and more numerous as the light dims. We believe life has been wiped clean from Jonkren, the northern continent. Yet still the cities mistrust each other and refuse aid, though resources are scarce for us all, with our land scoured by these things." The King sighed, looking down as he contemplated his next words. "We have little to offer as thanks. We have used much of our technology up in defence, or it choked on the dust, like our fixed-wing aircraft during the second year. Our airport is now just a sad reflection of what we used to be."

Zuri spoke, Smith translating for her through Finn's transmitter, "Your Majesty, we were happy to help. Your fallen soldiers have done your city proud. We couldn't stand by and do nothing. We would only ask to access one of your mines for our ship's repairs. We seek palladium."

"Palladium?" interrupted the Prime. "Yes, we had a mine, abandoned two wet seasons back during the second year of the dust's increase. I doubt much of the mining equipment will be intact."

"Is it a valuable resource, Heclite? How important will it be when the Boush are finally defeated?"

"It could be, Your Majesty. I believe it was an area of study for future technological developments. I do remember that the seam was rich."

"Hedging, Heclite, always hedging." The King turned his attention back to Zuri. "Heclite has asked for Hoplite Stremall to be your liaison. She will need a day or two to recover her strength, but I understand she is desperate to meet our saviours. I fear a medal will not be enough to placate her, and she is something of a hero in the city."

"Thank you, Your Majesty. Fighting beside her was an honour." Zuri paused.

Taking a chance, Finn. Go with me.

"We may also be able to provide you with something else in the future," she continued. "A possible gift from the Haven left on some of their planets. Technology they hid until the right time. Do we have permission to search for it? I make no guarantees, but it's possible they left a ship here."

"With our help?" said the Prime, eyes flicking between Zuri and the King.

"Yes, of course. This is your planet; we fully understand that you need to be cautious. Besides, we don't know where it's safe to explore." Zuri sucked in a breath, eyes on the King, as she took her first step into the world of diplomacy.

"I'll speak to Stremall, see what we can arrange," replied the King, a small smile playing across his lips.

"May we return to our ship while we wait?"

"Of course."

Zuri and Finn took that as a dismissal and bowed, turning to leave. Prime Heclite joined them as they left, her face relieved and posture buoyant. When they reached the end of the immense room, she turned to face them both.

"You know the Aven? Those that brought us here?" said the Prime, eager for their response.

"We know them as Haven, but yes, we have met them. Though time has not been kind," said Finn, receiving a nudge in the back from Zuri.

"How so? Their technology must be beyond our reckoning. All the cities hold them in great reverence, though none as much as ours. The temples pray for their return in rituals every day, more so since the Boush appeared. Are they coming for us? Will we ascend, as our city believes, to stand by their side and travel the Worlds Uncounted?" The glaze in Heclite's eyes sent out a warning that even Finn could see.

"We couldn't say. We can't speak for them, but we have briefly visited their home planet. I'm sorry, we are exhausted. Is it possible we could return to our ship and rest now?" asked Zuri, desperate to move away from the discomfort of the conversation. There was a trap there they needed to avoid, not deliberate, but a zealot was someone to be treated with caution when unsure of their premise.

"Yes, yes. This way."

CHAPTER 7

Palladium Mine Near New Halton

Yasuko adjusted the settings on the huge-wheeled truck as it emerged from the hold. It had survived the 33,000 odd years well, as had most of the mining equipment she'd stored after her last expedition. She remembered setting the nanobots on auto maintenance, but was still pleased to see them functioning so well. The remaining nanobots busied themselves reforming the cutting blades to slice through the accumulated debris on top of the mine.

Yasuko had analysed much of it, mainly plant husks and partial animal remains containing little nutrients. Discards from the slime mold's gradual destruction of the surrounding land. It was the level of cellular damage that disturbed her the most. This variant could easily break down all the husks into nutrients, yet chose not to, leaving low grade food behind on a voracious quest for fast, nutrient rich food it could rapidly absorb. For all her computing power, Yasuko struggled to understand why. She expected the answer to lie somewhere in the sporing they had witnessed on the northern continent. But the rapid growth, the hunger driving it to colonise, and the speed it moved at, all superseded her previous knowledge. An AI should not know fear, but the sheer momentum of these creatures paralysed her system analysis. All Yasuko could process was the emptiness in the north, and what it meant for life on the rest of the planet.

She switched her thoughts to the construction facility inside the ship. The development of Noah's request for armour adaptation was going well, but even so, she doubted it would last more than a minute under the chemical attack of the Boush. It was better, but marked the creatures as extremely dangerous in whatever form they came. Smith had asked about the light refracting camouflage she'd used on the ship and similar to the Stratan Armour back on Earth, but there simply wasn't time with all of Finn's requests for equipment. Besides, if the Boush were the principal threat, being seen wasn't the issue.

Yasuko froze, her systems suddenly freed by the distraction, and a single thought pushed itself forward, wrestling the others back, determined she should know.

The slime mold could change approach. Somehow it recognised when tactics were not working and adapted. Is it sentient?

Yasuko held the thought, stored it away to unpick later, hopeful that it would be a final piece to explain the extinction of life on half the world. At least the sensors had picked up the House responding to her most recent call, the low-frequency reply almost instant now she was in the atmosphere, and under the main cloud of the cosmic dust. Finn insisted they follow the signal as soon as possible, eager to be out doing something and hopefully resulting in them getting off the planet and home faster. Find the House, use it to locate the SeedShip, help the Bathsen humans and head home. Clean and simple in Finn's head.

With these humans, nothing is ever simple. Or clean. Or easy.

"We ready to go?" asked Finn, checking on his backpack for the third time. The incendiary grenades they'd swapped into their belt pouches, courtesy of Yasuko, should serve them well, though he'd popped in a couple of flashbangs just in case. The sidearm Yasuko had finally agreed to build them for fighting the mold on the city walls was also appreciated. He felt less naked now, and the additional power discs to boost their armour and weapons cheered him up, too. But he worried about their *weapons of choice.* They'd experimented with converting the armour piercing barrel to a flamethrower, but the material use had depleted the *weapons* in under two minutes. On Noah's suggestion, they settled on super heating air, reducing the range down to about two metres, but giving them much longer period of use. However, he wasn't sure that rapidly drying a flesh-eating mold was better than burning it. It just didn't feel right.

Like the hair dryer from hell, as Smith put it.

"Yep, ready," said Zuri, fixing her backpack to the new armour. She adjusted her open-faced helmet, the visor ready to pull down but enjoying the freedom the human bred biosphere afforded her, and with Yasuko's medical booster, they should be good for a while. She had also used Smith's updated language data to add a translator to all their radios.

"Me too," said Noah. Zuri had tried to dissuade him, but he was having none of it. He was struggling to understand her reluctance at the moment. The issue with Finn he understood, but she seemed agitated with him, as if he could do no right ever since they arrived on the planet. That nagging feeling wasn't going away, but now was not the time to face Zuri down. They had a job to do and as soon as they got on with it, the better. These people needed the SeedShip tech to fight the Boush and recover from the ecological mess their planet was in. The Boush had eaten almost everything on this part of the continent. It was only a matter of time before the unrelenting hunger drove it south.

The three of them stepped out of the ship. Yasuko watched them leave, experiencing a new emotion - trepidation. Humans were so fragile, and though the armour helped, since Noah's death she couldn't help but wonder how recklessly they threw themselves into danger for others. They seemed selfless, yet they talked constantly about the conflicts between their own kind. It made little sense at the beginning, but since Zuri had shared her grief, and taught Yasuko the meaning of friendship, she now saw that the bonds between them were forged by shared kinship. Something the greater body of humankind couldn't yet manage.

And Noah? The memory of his loss still caused pain despite his rebirth, or maybe because of it, a secret they chose to keep from him. But at least all three had discussed and agreed to the rebirth process before they set off, though it had its own pitfalls if done too often. The Haven Scientists' emotional connection with their fellow Haven, and towards humans for that matter, had fallen victim to their obsession with never dying.

Finn, Zuri and Noah jumped aboard the aircraft Hoplite Stremall gained for their mission. It presented as a hexacopter, drone like, with multiple small-bladed rotors in the corners of a hexagonal body. The cabin beneath having enough space for six soldiers, with a forward cockpit for the pilots. The Hoplite explained the air intakes were easier to modify against the dust that filled the atmosphere, and the number of rotors provided redundancy should they choke. Behind, a similar craft took off with a Phalanx of Sfendonatai, as the Hoplite called them. They appeared professional and highly trained; it was good to have backup for a change.

They lifted off in daylight and could view the devastation wrought by the Boush. They'd flattened the land, scouring every bush, tree or field in sight. Stripping the area of easily accessible nutrients and leaving the dried husks to rot. The Hoplite talked them through the ruined villages and wrecked mobile farmsteads. Nothing remained, everything laid waste or smashed. Amongst the debris, pulsating mold mounds twenty metres wide and high shivered in the light, clearly uncomfortable as they tried to cover themselves in the remains of their last meal.

None of them could look at Stremall with her tears flowing as she spoke, but it hardened their resolve to do what they could for the devastated land. After a few hours, as the rains started, the Hoplite pointed out the mountains in the distance. The

Seth they were called, a name also taken by the city a hundred kilometres southwest of them. Low and smooth compared to Earth's, with the minimal tectonic activity on the planet reflected in their form. Below them lay the foothills at the edge of what was once a plain, and their designated landing point. The immediate area appeared clear of the Boush, with Stremall explaining they may well be hiding from the light within the cave network that ran through the hills.

CHAPTER 8

Near The Seth Foothills

The black clad Phalanx took their positions around Zuri, Noah and Finn, with Stremall at their side. Their squad leader, Hoplite Tarn, had made it very clear he was in charge out here, and they were to do as he said. Finn had no argument for that. It was good to have experienced soldiers around him and reduce the burden of leadership. The aircraft had moved further out, away from the caves with a clear line of sight and, if need be, radar to pick up any Boush that may approach. For now, they were on their own, but evac was only ten minutes away. They had a three kilometre trek into the foothills, with Tarn not willing to risk a helicopter belay drop in the rising rain and wind.

"So how bad does the wet season get?" asked Noah, always curious to learn as they began their trek.

"We are over the worst," said Stremall, easing her hard armour chest plate aside as she scratched above her hip. "In the past, the land would regularly flood, the waters running off the mountains and enriching the plains. The growing season would follow, and our grasses would be rich and bountiful, our animals fat and the people well fed. However, we always put by for when the rains refuse to stop or the growing season falters. Our suns always seem to make life unpredictable, though the sea is our balance for when times are tough. But the dust has been here for the last four years, and during the worst times blocked the sunlight completely for weeks on end. The Boush soon followed, stripping the land bare. Only our spisym seed reserves and our sea food have kept the city going."

"And the Boush, we've been told they arose during the dust? Were they here before?" Finn and Zuri moved in closer with Noah's question, one they all wanted answering.

"They came with the dust, spores that settled on the northern continent. There were a few forms of Boush, slime molds I think we called them, already here. Small things that broke down the mulch and leaves in our forests. Our temple universities studied them and, from what I understand, they acted in similar ways but on a tiny scale…" Stremall trailed off, lost in her thoughts for a moment. "But these have taken so many of us, we were never a numerous people. We loved the wide-open spaces, and for many the nomadic way of life meant we had fewer children but even so…" Noah wanted to reach out, just a touch to communicate empathy, but couldn't as he didn't know how these people sought comfort from one another. "And the animals … so many species extinct as they feed on anything and everything, mercilessly."

"*We have a problem,*" said Smith. "*The helicopter pilots are on the line with Hoplite Tarn. They are under attack.*"

"Boush?" asked Finn.

"*No, other aircraft.*"

Finn strode over to Tarn, who stood still, the rest of his squadron eyeing the ravaged land warily as he listened and spoke into his own radio system.

"*One destroyed, sounds like a surface-to-air missile attack from a ground force, the other is being chased away by an armed helicopter. Tarn is calling it a Seth arsehole. I think that was the city nearby?*"

"Okay Smith, you're up. Full sensors on, I need to know who, what, why, where and when. No more lazing about, I think we are on our own for now."

"*Smith is at the wheel. Nothing on immediate sweep, but I'll get a feel for the lay of the land. Rain's about to ease, might help.*"

"Zuri, Noah, you getting this?"

"Yes, Corp." stated Noah, immediately taking the rear position and shadowing Zuri, his rifle at the ready.

"We still going for the House, Finn? Closer than any helicopter and it may provide cover," said Zuri.

"If we can get in. Don't forget the last one was under a rock face. Tarn will have to lead; he'll know local resources and evac potential. Be on your guard." Finn stepped into a crouch ready position, his team following suit as they awaited Tarn who spoke to his squad.

"He wants to go for the House, secure the resource for the city," said Smith.

Tarn signalled his men back to position, two at the rear, two at the front, and one on either side. Hoplite Stremall nodded as they moved out, Tarn explaining what was happening to her. She adjusted the strap around her shoulder, cradling the heavy-looking flame thrower she carried and quickly checked her flechette gun was strapped in its holster. Though holding a soldier's rank, Stremall trained as a city guard after retreating to the city under the onslaught of the Boush, a far cry from her nomadic life as a blacksmith following the Tramack animal herders across the plains. And right now, out here, she felt out of her depth.

These strangers? If they can help, then they need someone to stand by them.

The hillside ahead was stripped bare of grass and other plants, just the husks of unknown trees and rocks strewn around. Finn assessed ahead, very wary of being open to attack with no major cover. He felt an unease, the landscape not helping, but his innate sense of danger told him something was coming. They'd walked about half a kilometre when the nagging increased.

"Smith, Tarn got any thermal or night vision capability?"

"Some thermal I think using their sights, and their natural night

vision seems way better than ours. About ten years behind our tech back on Earth at a guess. I'm scanning, Finn. Nothing... wait, incoming mortar round."

Finn caught the whomp as Smith spoke, soon followed by another. Mortars were indiscriminate weapons, the shells explosive and often shrapnel laden, but this seemed a strange place to be using them.

"Mortar! Cover!" he shouted. Zuri and Noah reacted by hitting the dirt behind the husk of a tree trunk. Smith buzzed the message to Tarn, but his soldiers were already ducking for the floor having heard the mortar release. The shells hit the rocks and debris behind them, about five metres back, with dirt showering the Phalanx soldiers at the rear. Stremall stood frozen, eyes wide and shaking. An obvious target as the last figure standing.

"Move!" shouted Tarn, Smith's translation unneeded. Noah and Zuri took the Hoplite along with them, pulling her initially until her feet got moving, the heavy flamethrower hindering her already stiff progress. Gunfire rattled behind, Finn turned and took a knee behind a rock. He fired roughly above the source of the rounds, hoping to give the message to stay back.

"Smith?"

"It's a machine gun placement, heavily camouflaged and shielded by rocks. Up to the north on that small ridge. They could have taken us out, Finn. That was a deliberate miss. Judging by the heat signature, there's another to the south."

Another burst of gunfire hit the rocks and trunks just behind the group and in front of Finn, followed by a third from the southern position. Finn upped and followed the group; they were being herded like sheep and he had no idea why.

"Noah, Zuri, stay with Stremall. These attacks are designed to keep us moving. No shots at us, just around us."

"On it," came Zuri's reply.

Finn spun again, hitting the dirt and firing warning shots into the air. Whatever their plan was, they needed to send the message they were prepared to fire back. The whomp of the mortars rung out again. Finn rolled from his position and sprinted towards Tarn's men as the shells hit dirt behind him.

"Closer but a miss. Those mortars are about two hundred metres to the west, we are heading away from them."

Finn could see Tarn and his squad as he ran towards them, settled into cover amongst a pile of rocks and scorched branches, watching the downslope in an excellent defensive position. Zuri had a shaking Stremall pressed low to the ground, Noah kneeling beside on guard. In the old days they called it Shellshock. She wasn't ready to be back on duty; it was too soon. She'd clearly been through hell, and her mind and body couldn't cope right now, when the fulcrum of her daily life had changed so dramatically.

"Tarn, we are being herded up-slope. Anything up there?" asked Finn, Smith relaying.

"Mapping shows a large cave. On 3D it looks defensible. Used to be a show cave, tourist trap, built in steps and all that," replied Tarn. A show cave? Amongst the smashed and stripped landscape, a reminder of normal life. Finn couldn't imagine what hell these people had been through. "It's our best bet."

"I think that's where they want us to go. We head that way, and they'll spring whatever they have planned."

The sound of two more mortar shells echoed against the stone as they slammed into the ground nearby, accompanied by rapid gunfire strafing their rocks, chipping stone fragments into the air. Tarn's squad all ducked in unison, the shower of mud and stone spraying their helmets. Then, heads back up, they raised their rifles, firing back at unseen targets, their heavy rounds a mere warning rather than any real use. Their efforts were rewarded with more machine gun fire, this time centred on two of the black clad squad, shattering their protective rocks and forcing them back.

"Move, up-slope!" shouted Tarn, the heavy bombardment forcing his hand.

"Go with Zuri, Noah, and take Stremall. I'll cover the retreat. But don't follow them into that cave unless Smith says so. Whatever happens."

Finn and two of Tarn's rearguard knelt against the rocks, firing through the dust and flying fragments to keep their assailants back. After a few bursts, one tapped him on the arm, pointing him towards Zuri and the others. Finn slapped him on the shoulder, nodded and set off, aiming for the next cover position to allow them to follow.

"Finn, Zuri, I'm getting multiple thermal signatures in that cave, and to the left and right, there are probably more. Heavily camouflaged."

Finn reached the cover point, torn between pursuing his squad and the responsibility towards the soldiers below him. He took up the retreat cover point; he had to rely on Tarn and the others to do their job while he did his. Finn dived to the dirt, raising his rifle to looking down the sight. His *weapon* focussed in on the mortar Smith had described, smoke rising from it as another shell launched into the air. Two soldiers, one male the other female, in combat fatigues and helmets, appeared in his scope, prepping the next shell.

No one has died yet. Am I the one to start the killing? I do not know these people, or who the enemy really is.

The shell crashed between the two soldiers below, the explosive shrapnel peppering their armour and clothes, ripping through to the soft tissue underneath. Finn fired, the two energy bolts fizzing across the distance to smash against the mortar, twisting its barrel and forcing it careering backwards. No remorse, his third and fourth shots seared into their camouflaged shoulders. They might live or they might not, but it ended the barrage for now.

"Finn, I think it's us they're after," shouted Zuri over the radio.

CHAPTER 9

Seth Foothills

Zuri held back, as Tarn and his four remaining squad members headed towards the cave mouth. To the left was a small, sheer cliff, about eight metres high, but there was no time for climbing. To the right, a recent rockfall blocked the slope before another small and climbable cliff, but they'd be sitting ducks up there. The entrance itself was low and wide, a deep blackness within and Zuri could sense movement. Flipping her visor, the Heads Up Display rapidly adjusted for the light and heat change at the cave mouth. On the roof, she picked out low-temperature signatures pulsing in unison, recognising them instantly, adding to her resolve. Below them, a jumble of possibly eight to ten human figures.

"Noah, back. Not the cave." As she spoke, the human signatures moved, and the thunder of heavy gunfire ripped the air asunder. Blood plumes splattered Tarn and his squad's heat images as their armour gave out under the barrage. It was a slaughter, a trap sprung with the intent to kill.

She pulled Stremall back towards the downslope, Noah providing covering fire towards the cave, his own HUD and *weapon* supporting his aim. His accuracy confirmed by the agonised shouts as the searing energy bolts hit home. From Zuri's left a figure sprang from amongst the branches and earth, its camouflaged uniform green and grey, the heavy weapon in their hand aimed in her direction.

"Edo pera!" echoed loudly from the cliff behind. The

ambushing soldier swivelled, instinctively responding to the call, before his body convulsed. His trembling finger jammed down on the trigger, releasing a swirling nest of wire and heavy metal balls crackling with electricity as they soared past Zuri.

"Finn, I think it's us they're after," shouted Zuri over the radio, eyes searching for whoever had taken out the soldier. Flicking her HUD back to thermal, she caught the signature of another rising from the ground. Bringing her own rifle up, Noah beat her to it, his bolts slamming into the torso and sending the soldier spiralling back into their hole.

"Edo pera!" Turning, Zuri's HUD caught a very slight temperature difference against the right-hand cliff face. Switching to visual, she immediately set off in that direction. There, against the cliff, grey as the stone itself, knelt a beckoning figure. Dragging Stremall with her, she noted Noah following, but kept her eyes on the signalling girl as she faded in and out against the background of the cliff. Gun fire clattered behind, and she recognised the heavy rounds of Tarn's weapons. Someone must be putting up a fight back there, but she had no time to look.

Zuri reached the cliff. The waiting teenage girl, patterned in shades of grey on her skin and clothes, took her by the arm, dragging her back behind the edge of the rockfall. She pointed towards a small opening in the cliff, just big enough for them to crawl through. Zuri pushed Noah ahead, sending him in and taking no heed as he tried to argue, with Stremall behind, so lost in herself she followed robotically. Zuri turned, scanning the cave mouth for any sign of Finn, torn between keeping Noah and Stremall safe, and the need to find him.

"Finn! Finn!" she bellowed down the radio.

"They have him, Zuri. Go, get out. He's ali-" said Smith, a roar of static ensued, followed by silence.

Anger boiled from the pit of Zuri's stomach. They had attacked no one, yet here they were, once again under fire. She moved to leave, her trigger finger straining, when the small grey hand pulled at her elbow.

"Edo pera," the girl said, pulling again. Zuri stopped, looking at the hole behind her.

Me and mine.

Zuri allowed herself to be pulled towards the hole, pushing through to the narrow tunnel beyond, just wide and high enough for her backpack to scrape through. Two metres down, halfway, she remembered her HUD and switched to night vision, Noah's face coming into view as he peered back at her. When she finally made it, he helped her up into the dry cave beyond.

"I've checked. There's no Boush in here within range. It appears very dry, probably not to their liking," Noah said.

The girl's arms came through the tunnel next; she slithered out, turning lithely to face back down it and yanking on a metal bar wrapped with heavy string. Zuri heard the keystone fall, realisation piercing her heart as the tunnel collapsed in a rumble of dust and stone.

CHAPTER 10

Seth Foothills

The bola wrapped around Finn's legs, the stones intertwining and forcing him to the floor as he overbalanced. Electricity surged along the wires, crackling but impotent against his ceramic armour. Finn's servos worked to stretch and snap the restraining cable, but the wires held fast. Swiftly giving up, he searched for his rifle lost in the fall, and scrambled towards it, dragging his entangled legs behind him. A uniformed leg kicked out at the we*apon*, sending it across the ground towards a pile of branches and browned grass.

"There's eight of them, Finn, all heavily armed."

"Finn! Finn!" came Zuri's voice over the radio, followed by a swift kick into Finn's ribs.

"They have him, Zuri. Go get out. He's ali-"

A hand snaked out and ripped the mike off his helmet, snapping it in two, causing static to roar in his ears. The buzzing soon died away, and with the radio silent, they sliced his helmet chinstrap and threw it aside. Another kick, and Finn lay still, the message loud and clear. He lifted his arms, placing them behind his head, not relaxing but showing he would stop struggling. They wrapped more wire around his wrists, pulling tight against his tensed muscles, recognising his attempts to keep it loose. Finn felt hands all over his back, his pack straps sliced, with the pouch belt soon following, and finally the holster for his sidearm removed. The searching hands were quick and experienced. His knife, the replacement after losing Corporal Lumu's kukri on Haven, swiftly followed.

They flipped Finn over; he chose not to resist as it seemed futile. With the enemy soldiers now in his view he counted four of them, all wearing camouflaged fatigues and combat armour that wouldn't look out of place on Earth. Their weapons a mix of heavy and lighter rifles. If Finn squinted, he could imagine he was back home. Their expressions were grim, and Finn recognised the soot staining over their hands and faces.

They talked at him, nudging with their feet as he shrugged at their words. A few more rough prods and he spoke.

"Listen fellas, I have no clue what you're saying and the only one who does isn't here right now." Finn tensed, waiting for the follow through, but no more kicks came. They babbled between themselves before bringing over a long pole and slipping it between his tied legs and arms. The soldiers lifted Finn off the ground.

Please let Zuri have got away.

Placing the pole on their shoulders, they turned to walk down the slope and Finn caught sight of Tarn's squad, cut down and bloodied, scattered across the mouth of the cave. No mercy given once they'd separated their targets from the Phalanx. He hurriedly scanned the killing zone, a sense of relief washing over him. Zuri and Noah were absent from the carnage, and that, combined with the last messages over the radio, allowed a seed of hope to grow. Maybe Stremall was with them, her body also not present amongst the pile of dead.

The soldiers gathered his stuff, visored helmet and rifle included, and they began the painful journey back down the slope.

A hunted animal, trapped and on its way to the pot. It's not been a good day.

Finn ignored the swaying and the ache running through his

shoulders. He focussed on the flex of his shoulder and elbow servos, giving them just enough juice to take the pressure off his joints for a few minutes at a time. Designed for sudden movement, they were not so happy when locked into an active holding position. Finn added that to the list of improvements, that and a set of inbuilt wire cutters. Over the crunch of tree husks and fractured rocks, helicopter engines and the swoosh of rotor blades made their presence known. Finn turned his head, risking the strain on his neck to catch sight of the machine. It was similar in design to New Halton's, with four larger sets of blades rather than six. Another hovered above, short wings bristling with mini missiles.

They tossed Finn to the ground with no gentleness or care. All eight soldiers throwing their equipment on board before returning to lift him onto the basket cradle sat on its landing gear. As the engines roared, Finn could feel the helicopter lift, and the moment he'd been waiting for. When it reached three metres, he activated the servos up to full power on his wrist control. His legs jerked against the wire, knees straining to push back and stretch it beyond breaking point. Finn relaxed, then strained again, only to be met with a rifle butt crashing against his forehead, and the deep black of unconsciousness.

CHAPTER 11

Cave Complex, Seth Foothills

The grey girl tugged at Zuri, pulling her away from the collapsed tunnel. She continued to speak, her words urgent, but they meant little to Zuri and Noah, with the translator keyed only to New Halton's language. Zuri's mind whirled. Cut off from Finn, though he was alive according to Smith, she worried over where they would take him. The spaceship must have been the reason for the kidnap attempt. They could have been spotted on entry into the atmosphere, or word had spread about their actions at New Halton. Whatever the reason, this trap had deliberately separated them, and the killing of Tarn's people ruthless and calculated.

A gentle glimmer of residual light refracted off the surrounding cave walls. With their HUD night vision activated, they walked unhindered by the near dark as they followed the girl. Zuri could see Noah ahead, leading the increasingly responsive Stremall down the tunnel.

One thing less to worry about.

To Zuri, she was an interesting enigma. She was likely in her late teens, with skin and clothes covered in a grey dust that matched the stone around them. Strapped to her thigh was a sidearm, some form of stun weapon from what she'd witnessed. Across her back was a grey pack with multiple pockets, ropes and clips attached. She moved through the tunnels with ease, even without the benefit of electrically enhanced night vision. Her eyes were large, like the other people on the planet, but

Zuri understood from her movements that she was more than just familiar with the route they took. An urgency to her stride, and with the babble of words increasing, she took them from junction to junction. After thirty minutes, she stopped at another rockfall, running her hands along the inner wall nearest to it. Zuri heard a motor kick in, the rockfall moving backwards and to the side as a complete piece, swinging like a door. Beyond, the natural cave ceased, the walls carved and smooth with the floor a carpet of moss. Lamps from the ceiling glowed, faint, but enough after the dimness of the cave to let them see. The girl beckoned them in.

Zuri stepped through the threshold. The corridor was short with an elaborate stone carved balustrade standing six metres further on. Beyond that a void, the blackness streaked with veins of twinkling lights. She walked through to the cavern, her hands trembling as they rested on the cold stone rail. Galleries arrayed concentrically above and below, all hung with a swirl of green plants, life that had been so absent from the world above. Sparkling waterfalls leapt out into the void, tumbling down to the shimmering lake below. They refracted the sparkled light with rainbows pervading the air, water droplets dancing to gravity's tune. It was stunning, and the size was so difficult to take fully in. Noah's hands set upon the rail beside her, his demeanour as awestruck as hers, mouth wide and sounds of joy slipping out, as uncontrolled as his emotions.

Zuri turned to usher Hoplite Stremall over, but she stood by the girl, her arms hiding her as she washed naked in a waterfall. The stone dust scrubbed clean to leave an almost albino skin beneath.

"Don't turn round, Noah. Keep looking at the pretty lights." Noah made to turn; his curiosity piqued by Zuri's tone, but she pushed him back. "It's best this way, trust me."

"Uh, okay," he replied. "Any clue where we are? No one's mentioned this place at all, and I can't believe what I'm seeing. It just doesn't compute."

"Nope," said Zuri, relieved the girl had finished and was dressing in a multi-coloured set of new clothes, though she had no idea where they had appeared from. The contrast against her skin was startling, and a weight seemed to have been lifted off the girl with a glorious smile replacing the anxious frown.

"Noah, when you turn around the grey girl will be completely different, hard to believe she's the same one." Noah turned, as taken aback at the sight of the girl's transformation as he was with the glory of the cavern behind him.

"Ela edo," the girl said, taking Zuri by the hand and leading her down the stairway carved centrally through the galleries. They followed, Hoplite Stremall now fully aware after her stupor, and walking beside Noah down the curved steps, eyes beginning to soak in the surrounding wonders. Noah could see the anxiety recede as the stiffness to her movements eased, though his experience with Finn taught him it never left completely.

"How... How did we get here?" Stremall asked. "And where is here? I remember the bombs, and the gunfire and a Ghost, but..."

"Not a ghost," said Noah, "a girl covered in grey dust."

"Yes, a Ghost. The Ghosts Within lived in the foothill caves, though we assumed them all dead after the Boush arrived. The mountains and the hills were the first to be hit by the spores floating over from the northern continent. They were a simple people, their population sparse even before the Boush. My people flew over and checked the area, trying to help in the early days, but the Boush overran everything, and the Ghosts were not to be found."

"Well, I think you might be in for a surprise," said Zuri as they reached the level below. Hundreds of children sat on cushions, partitioned off by green bushes, watching viewscreens or listening to the adults at the front. It was silent because of the headphones they wore, the only noise the tap of writing upon computer tablets. Their clothes were a breath-taking myriad of colours, making the room feel bright and alive. The children's smiles a million miles away from the scorched earth above. "I think your Ghosts may well have been hiding in the dark."

"Ela edo," the girl repeated, leading them towards the centre of the gallery, a hundred metres distant, with the row upon row of children being replaced by empty play areas and a small swimming pool. Near the centre column, a fountain danced to a gentle rhythm of music played by a cross-legged man on a plush golden cushion, an electronic flute at his lips. The girl approached him, a smile still upon her lips, speaking in a low murmur as the man stopped playing to listen. When she finished, he stood, stretching his legs and feeling his stiff joints.

"Ah, welcome," he said in the language of New Halton. "Kinsik wishes you well. She apologises, but she missed most of the lessons on your language when her mother took ill." The man reached out and wrapped his arms around the girl in a warm embrace. His skin was as olive as Stremall's, not the white softness of Kinsik's, who smiled at them and ran off towards the school.

"I am Wendyll. As you may tell, I am from New Halton stock, though I have lived here for over four years now. Since the spores first came." Wendyll's face briefly spoke of pain before he continued, "Kinsik tells me she rescued you from a Seth Phalanx. However, she believes many others died. Would you like to explain yourselves? You two are not from New Halton or anywhere else I've heard of by your appearance."

"We were here to find something," said Stremall, wary but honest, "that these two ...erm... space travellers are seeking. They helped rescue the city from the Boush. The slime was in a feeding frenzy and the city was about to be overrun. Their ship burnt the Boush, and Zuri and Finn stood by my side as we fought off the rest." Wendyll nodded throughout, his eyes darting from Zuri to Noah. "They have offered us the chance to gain technology to survive the mold and the dust, to recover and rebuild."

Zuri watched Wendyll intently, adamant in her own mind that he already knew what they were seeking. Not only knew about it, but it surrounded them. That was the secret of the Ghosts Within. They had flowered from what they had already learned and kept it to themselves.

Akili ni mali. Knowledge is wealth.

"And this technology, you want to share it with New Halton?" asked Wendyll, his gaze steady upon Zuri. She felt the examination down to her soul. This unassuming man was as sharp as a tack. Zuri held his gaze as she considered which way to go.

"My aim is to share it with your world. It is of no use to save one city when others fall, nor is it morally right to do so. The army of Seth attacked us today, took our friend. Are they worthy of saving in your opinion?"

Back at you, mister flute playing, soothsayer man. I want my Finn back.

Wendyll gave Zuri a rueful smile. "We are sparring. There seems little point in continuing it. These people have benefitted from the caverns they discovered here many thousands of years ago. The halls of our Gallery had already been carved. The Ghosts learned how it was done through trial and error, and have been adding to it ever since. Their ingenuity is only bound by human imagination and the machines they make. They also discovered that time below caused their skin to burn above, hence the stone powder, and the Ghosts Within were born from strangers' imagination. However, most of what you see around us in terms of computer technology they stole from the cities, learnt about it and improved upon it. Here we are hidden from the Boush and the failures caused by petty squabbles between the cities." Zuri caught Stremall nodding in agreement. There was no magic to tablets and viewscreens.

"But you stay hidden while they die above? Why not help?" butted in Noah, angry lines creasing the corner of his eyes. "You have all this and yet you do nothing?"

"That is easier said than done, young man. There is no magic button to press that will rid us of that scourge. And if we open our doors, the Boush will pour in. The religious arguments and politics that prevent the cities from cooperation are delivered from behind high walls. If the slime mold gets in here, the end would come quickly."

Zuri raised her hands to ask for calm, "When they found these caverns, were the ceilings low and the door handles wide? As if the inhabitants were short and squat?"

"Yes, yes. The Aven, we believe they extended what was already here. Beyond the ridiculous bunkum each city believes, they were real. The Ghosts found paintings and sculptures in the upper gallery."

"What we're looking for will have a metal wall or doorway, blue-hued and smooth. That here too?" Wendyll's face told her all she needed to know. "So, it's my turn. No more sparring. If, and I mean if, I can find the Haven technology, where do you stand?"

Wendyll dropped his eyes to the floor, a half-smile on his lips coloured by a stiffness in his posture. Zuri could feel the man's tension.

He told me much without concern until I mentioned involving others.

"Kinsik was not at that cave by accident, and I bet you have other watchers out there. I think you knew our ship was here, and I think you were expecting us, or more likely the Aven. Everyone needs that tech; everyone has a right to survive. What I seek is probably not here in your people's home, but the way to finding it is. Together we can understand the link and then share it with everyone, the Ghosts Within included. What you do after that is your decision. But I want something in return."

CHAPTER 12

Approaching Seth City

The wind rush drew Finn back into the conscious world, his suit preventing most of the cold, but the skin on his face stung with the bitterness in the air and the lashing rain. His nose hurt, and if he ever saw Zuri again on this crazy world, then she could at least find some joy in his newly improved face. Finn adjusted in the cradle, twisting to keep the rain out of his eyes and to get a view below. They were approaching a city, the walls six metres lower than New Halton's, but here they set the flamethrowers high on cranes that reached over the battlements. He counted at least six per battlement, with four long walls to defend and no ocean at their back. Below, house-sized Boush gathered, a gelatinous sea of yellow and green that pulsed menacingly across the barren land. Finn guessed at thirty of the huge throbbing creatures, merging under the rain darkened sky. It was near dusk; they were hungry, and they could taste the city on the air. It wasn't looking good.

So why am I here?

As they passed over the walls, Finn could see the landing pad, the other helicopter already in place being refuelled, probably on their way out to battle the Boush the best they could. He wished them luck, despite his bruised and battered face and losing his companions. No one should lose their loved ones in this way. They all fought for a cause, a belief that they were right. People sometimes become blinded to the truth by those they serve, or so desperate that they make poor decisions. If it was his people facing the rasp of those pseudopods melting flesh and bone, then his decision making would be clouded too. Just look at how he struggled to cope when Zuri, or even Noah lately, faced danger.

Molds? These things are predators. Emotionless monsters.

An updraft bounced off the landing pad towards the rotor blades, jolting the helicopter. The pilot compensated, bringing the four-engined machine down in the centre of the pad. Finn heard the soldiers disembark; orders barked in a language he had no hope of understanding, but he could sense their exhaustion. If it was anything like he had faced at New Halton, there would be long hours of pain and loss before the night was out. Brothers in arms would fall like those of Hoplite Stremall, the last of her squad upon the wall, prepared to burn her own soldiers to see out their dying wish. No wonder she had frozen out there today. That horror would be with her for the rest of her life.

Two soldiers lifted his cradle from the helicopter landing gear, taking either end and carrying him to the brick-built building by the side of the pad. They opened the door, setting him down on the floor beside a functional desk and chair occupied by a huge bald man, his eyes watery and blue, a sneer already set in place. Finn knew what was coming. This wasn't a soldier; it was the face of a politician.

This should be fun.

Finn jumped the gun. "There's no point. You can't understand me, and I can't understand you. Helmet," Finn shouted, "I need my helmet with the translator in it." Finn waggled his head in a forlorn hope he'd be understood.

Well, it did before they broke the damn thing.

The politician rose from his seat, coming round the desk to kneel next to Finn. The soldiers were immediately wary, rifles in hand. He spoke with the same rapid tongue the soldiers used. It wasn't quite the same as New Halton's, but Finn recognised similar rhythm and patterns. His frustration grew. If only he could talk to them, explain.

The man reached for something on his desk, bringing over a small tablet screen. He flipped it to show Finn a fuzzy shot of Yasuko's ship, the top half only because of the light camouflage. He spoke animatedly again, jabbing his finger at the fire emanating from its engines. Subsequently, he flicked the photo over to show a snapshot of her first strafing run across the southern wall. When Zuri and he had supported Stremall, just after the Boush attack forced her to burn her own squad. What a thing to have to do. More finger jabbing continued, Finn trying to communicate, but at a loss.

The door opened and a woman in her mid-fifties walked in, another tablet in hand. It was the first woman he'd seen since capture; every soldier and pilot so far had been male. She was immediately subservient in manner, her posture and facial expression masking any emotion other than compliance. The politician shouted at her, pointing to Finn. She tapped at the tablet, a variety of words came from its speakers, but none were in English. He tried to stay calm but wrapped in wire, freezing cold and laying on a floor while being jabbered at, wasn't helping. Finn shouted, wrestling his hands in the air against the wire, causing lesions and blood to well. The woman backed off, clearly afraid of him as well as the man at her side.

One soldier stretched across and hit Finn on the side of the head, not hard, a tap to remind. He brought his hands down and shouted in frustration. A few more words from the politician and they heaved him up off the floor, dragging him through an internal door and down some steps. Finn's wired feet thumped against each one on the way down, but he felt nothing, numb after being trussed up so long. Eventually they passed a few cell doors, accompanied by pitiful keening, empty of all emotion except hopelessness. They dumped Finn onto the stone floor with one soldier kneeling on his back, a gun to his neck as the other cut the wire from his legs and stripped off his armour.

Finn suppressed the urge to fight back. These men knew what they were doing and there'd be a hole in his head if he even flinched. The soldiers lifted and threw him into the last cell, slamming the metal door shut. A jabber of words tumbled through the window, drawing Finn's attention to the wire cutters waggling through them. He dragged himself up against the nearest wet stone wall. Leaning over, he offered his bloodied hands, the sharp cutters shearing through the wire and allowing the blood to rush back. Finn held back the agony, refusing to give them the pleasure of his pain, then slumped to the floor.

CHAPTER 13

Upper Gallery, City Within, Seth Foothills

Zuri placed her hands on the metal wall, feeling the warmth and a distant pulse in response. Around her, the plastic sealed paintings of Havenhome hung upon the walls. The representations appeared to be gatherings, with formal poses around intricately carved slab tables the norm. She noted the recurrent members by the adornments on their scales, a tradition that lasted beyond the Great Fall triggered by Scientific Officer Xxar - the genocide he enacted in response to the Restoration Faction attack on the Orbital Station.

What came as a surprise was the huge cityscape that adorned one wall. Beautifully hand drawn, the buildings spread as far as the eye could see. A distant cry from what she saw of the planet, it appeared crowded, with each building fighting for space on the ground and in the air. But somehow it captured a love, maybe a respect, for the city. She found it strangely moving, though knowing the city and its people's fate may have affected that feeling. Below, clearly suffering through the years, were life-sized statues of Haven, their scale adornments missing, presumably rotted, but distinguishable from one another despite their age.

Behind her, Wendyll stood, arms crossed, watching her with a mix of curiosity and impatience. If he'd been expecting an immediate response, he was mistaken. Zuri had been stroking the wall in different places for the past ten minutes, hoping to find a recess that her visor could not pick out. On Earth, the

House responded to Smith. However, *!Nias's* people had been interfering with its AI beforehand. Later, she had gained entry to their ship, but Yasuko had talked about her not 'yet' being designated a SeedShip, rather being primed ready for that role.

"Well? I assume this is what you expected." Wendyll said.

"Yes. Well, yes and no. I've only seen one before. The entry plaque is with Finn, the man who we lost to the Seth soldiers, the man I want back. I suspect we'll need to rescue him and his equipment, if we are to gain entry."

"That's a little convenient, isn't it? You offer us a way to destroy the Boush and free our planet, but not proof. In return, you want help to free the one person who can open it. I feel I am being played here, Zuri. I thought you were more intelligent than that." Zuri took Wendyll's demeanour with a pinch of salt. She'd just offered him cake, only to present him with an empty plate.

Zuri reached around her back, pulling the rifle out and into her hands. Wendyll visibly flinched, raising a flash of a warrior's smile from her. She had seen no guards or soldiers during their route to the House door, and he appeared less than keen as she flipped the *weapon* in her hands.

"It's okay, chill. See these?" Zuri pointed to her plaque copy. "You have any around the cavern?" Wendyll moved closer, reaching out and touching the plaque.

"Yes, the Ghosts have tiled the fountain with them. Why?"

"These have many uses for the Haven, including as data storage units. A few are used as keys." Zuri avoided mentioning the full body and memory copies of people stored on some versions. With the irony of the metal plaques retaining ghost copies once the power ran out, just a little too close to home in the cavern.

Ghosts within.

"Can we prize them off, see if any will work?"

Wendyll sighed, but nodded in response, calling over some of the curious Ghosts hovering at the edge of the room. A few words and they disappeared, returning thirty minutes later with ten of the metallic plaques, tile cement stuck to their backs.

Zuri piled them next to the wall, taking a deep breath as she picked the first one up and placed it on the smooth metal. A blue flicker swiftly died, but it heralded a little hope.

"I saw that, Zuri. That, at least, was something," Wendyll said.

"I think we should try charging them, put an extra power disc on the back and leave them for a while before trying again," said Noah. Zuri nodded agreement and by the time they had checked the entire pile, they had two on charge. She handed one to Wendyll, offering him the opportunity to place it on the wall. As he did so, he felt a tingle run through his fingers, a small surge of electromagnetic current. The key glowed with a much stronger light, and he yanked his hand back, leaving behind the skin from his fingertips. Fascinated, he watched the skin absorb into the metal. Turning to show Zuri, her broad smile met his response.

"How? What?" Wendyll said, staring at the wall and then at his fingertips.

"You've been sampled," said Noah. "But no flashing lights, Zuri." They waited a little longer, but no response was forthcoming.

"Put your entire hand on, palm down. It may sample all the hand, possibly put a hole in your wrist. It's a shock, but it's okay." Wendyll followed Noah's instructions, the tingle spreading through his entire palm, and he felt a sharp pain in the wrist that swiftly subsided. A blue light flashed; the skin absorbed.

"Rejected, bioanalysis complete. Microorganism threshold surpassed," sounded a mechanical voice, using the language of New Halton. Wendyll reached out again, but Noah took his hand, pulling it away.

"Yasuko, our...crew mate, told us that the humans were

seeded on Bathsen to make the planet bio ready for the Haven to colonise. They wouldn't survive the illnesses if they breathed the atmosphere or ate locally grown food. You were put here to change all of that for them. But it wasn't supposed to be for this long, a few thousand years at most, but they suffered a tragedy on their planet over 30,000 years ago. The system isn't working correctly, maybe because of the time delay. However, I also think the scientists hadn't finished the preparations when they were recalled. Here, on your planet, those microorganisms have developed beyond the system's parameters."

"Then what now?"

Zuri took over. "Now we get Finn, recover the key plaque and get you in. We have at least proven that the wall reacts. Is that enough for you?"

"Yes," responded Wendyll, staring at his hand, "it is."

CHAPTER 14

Prison Cell, Seth City

Finn awoke to banging on his cell door, with words tumbling in as incomprehensible now as they'd been when he first arrived. However, he recognised the voice, the woman who'd tried to converse with him earlier. Groggy, his wrists and calves still complaining, he got up from the filthy cot bed and made his slow way to the door. The grey-haired woman still showed a glimmer of fear, though because of Finn or her apparent subservience to men, he did not know. When he was finally at the door, her tone altered, and she carefully offered papers through the window with a set of waxed crayons.

Ah, the old-fashioned way. I'll be drawing cave paintings next.

Finn looked through the papers. She had already drawn their ship and the engine fire, followed by an arrow and a low-walled city, with flamethrowers on cranes. The last picture was of the Boush, an enormous cross over them and fire by the side. Even Finn could work out the meaning, but was at a complete loss over the kidnapping and murder used to get his help.

Why didn't they just ask the King? Surely, they have direct lines of communication. Are we humans just a lost cause?

Finn drew a picture of his helmet. At least it looked like his helmet to him, and a big tick against the crossed-out Boush, handing his pictures over to the woman. He pointed to the picture and back to his head, drawing its shape in the surrounding air. The woman shrugged, so he tried again, using his hands in a talking gesture and pointing to the picture. The light lit up in her eyes and face; she ran off with a swirl of soot and smoke in the air behind her.

A few minutes later, Finn heard the door clatter open above, and then steps being jumped. He eyed the door as the woman's soot-stained face reappeared, sweat and blood pouring from her forehead in unison. Keys jangled, scrabbling in the lock before she stopped as one turned. The woman shouted through the window, pointing at the back wall. Finn moved away from the door, a crack of hope in reach now his message was getting through to someone. The helmet clattered to the floor, with the useless microphone dangling from the socket swinging as the door slammed shut and the key turned. Finn couldn't blame her, no risks. Sliding across, he picked up the helmet, relieved to see Smith still attached to the back. Placing it upon his head, he waggled the broken mic in vain.

"It's okay Finn, I can hear you. I've adjusted my auditory sensors so I can pick up the vibrations. Nothing else to do."

"Can you translate their language?"

"It's a strange dialect, but yes."

Finn glanced across at the woman through the cell window. Her contorted face greeted him as she stared back, mouth open in a silent scream. He sped across to the door, to see the hated, pulsating Boush, wrapped around her legs. Its pseudopods reaching up to her waist, rasping at material and flesh, flinging out tendrils to melt her arms and shoulders. The agonised scream finally rattled loose, rising in pitch, scraping across Finn's nerve endings. Every ounce of pain hammered into his soul as he clung onto his sense of *self*. An unnamed woman's tear-filled eyes locked with his as she reached out, sliding the cell window shut as a hunger filled tendril shot out towards him.

CHAPTER 15

Underground River, City Within, Seth Foothills

Zuri rechecked her backpack and then the waterproof bag the Ghosts Within had given her. Someone had carefully wrapped food parcels, assuring her and Noah that the algae and moss were edible, and to pay no mind to the soulless colour of the dried fish. Noah was not so sure. He was never a lover of exotic foodstuffs, and Yasuko's attempts at widening his palate with her printed foods never went down well. Admittedly, Zuri had passed on the Haven delicacy of green and gold Shtrym worms herself, despite Yasuko's assurances.

Kinsik sat at the bow of the boat amongst all her other equipment, her grey powder reapplied. She now sported a rifle similar to those the Phalanx carried, and Zuri was in no doubt she could use it, watching the ease with which she checked it over. At the rear of the six-metre-long boat, the steersman sat greyed-up and surrounded by a collection of metal poles of differing lengths. They'd chosen the man, Sundar, because of the smattering of New Halton words he knew. Enough to manage the two-day trip along the underground river that Wendyll assured them flowed most of the way to Seth. He'd told them it was how Seth Foothills got their name, before the river was lost to a sinkhole millennia ago. The combination of Haven built tunnels and caverns it now followed diverged slightly from the original route, but it was safer than travelling on the surface.

Stremall sat in the middle, insisting she needed to help rescue Finn, that it was her duty placed upon her by the King. Zuri would have preferred her not to be there. She was a loose cannon and, after freezing during the Seth Phalanx ambush, one that was a probable liability. Despite Zuri's protestations, she sat with the heavy flame thrower across her lap.

"Sundar will wait with the boat at the landing point. The Ghosts used it often enough before the Boush, when they thieved Seth City's tech. It should still be sound. Sundar will set you a time frame when you arrive, and he'll return upstream using the electric motor after it has passed. The current is mild along the route with the rains easing, so you should have little trouble. You have the transmitter if you have to return on your own. Use that near the cave Kinsik rescued you from and we'll pick it up. And... Zuri, Kinsik is my stepdaughter. She's as headstrong as her mother and loves the surface world nearly as much. Please..." Zuri reached out and took Wendyll by the arm and, looking in his eyes, she squeezed his arm and nodded.

Message received; we all have ones to watch out for on this trip.

Wendyll moved nearer to Kinsik, embracing her before exiting the boat, his heart racing as he waved goodbye. Sundar fired up the electric motor on the outboard, and taking the rudder, he steered them to the middle of the shallow river as they left the light of the small cavern behind. Kinsik set a lantern up on the bow, the soft glow warming the darkness and causing a skittering of multi-legged creatures to rush from the light along the cavern walls. The occasional soft plop of the river heralded those that never quite made it. Zuri's mind raced back to the Data Storage building on Havenhome, and the explosion of life there. Shudders tingled down her spine, and she took stolen glances towards Noah, before locking the memories away.

"Did you hear that, Noah?" she whispered through the radio. "I'm giving you her back to keep an eye on, and I'll watch Stremall. You need to make her part of the team, mould her to work with us rather than trying to run ahead. Get me?"

"Yeah, okay. On it." Noah moved forward, flipping his visor

down to scan thermally ahead, before sitting near Kinsik. Not the most socially adept, he felt more than a little out of his depth, so he fell back on his usual approach, curiosity.

"Hi... err... any fish in the river?"

CHAPTER 16

In Orbit, Planet Bathsen

"Any readings?" asked Zzind, shuffling in the captain's chair that she had never quite got used to. Ship had made a few adjustments, but it just felt too big for her. Giving up, she stood and approached the view screen, planet Bathsen completely filling it. Likely a human planet, seeded by her kind and left to brew a bacterial and viral soup, ready for colonisation.

"Yes, there's palladium on the planet. There are traces in the atmosphere, though they are not huge. I doubt it is in much productive use on this planet," Ship replied.

"Anything else I need to know?"

Like, are there humans? Is this their home world? Is that human controlled ship down there?

"I am a non-suggestive system, Zzind, as well you know. I will interpret your question as always based on the previous experience and parameters I have about you. Yes, there are humans. Yes, the Explorer ship is down there. Beyond that, we would need to enter the atmosphere to gather more data, but I doubt this is the home world. The conurbation spread is very low, though the dust cloud is affecting all sensors." Ship sighed inwardly, it had never chafed at the Haven Convention bonds, always happy to serve its crew with little need to explore any *deeper* meanings unlike some of the other AIs it conversed with. But these last few weeks with Zzind had driven it to distraction. Her zealous and unthinking approach to life made it consider who was the actual slave on the spaceship. Why did humans feel the need to wrap themselves up in problems, seeking reasons and purpose when they could simply just *be*?

"How long will the dust be hitting the planet? When we came through, the cloud seemed much thicker than what's streaming across right now," Zzind asked.

"I'd estimate another week before Bathsen fully passes through the tail end, then there'll be a clear run before a few, much less dense, residual clouds. I don't even think they'll do much to diminish the light on the planet, but the meteor showers will still be as spectacular."

Zzind considered Ship's reply, very aware they needed to mine palladium after emerging from the Node straight into a dense mass of the cosmic dust. Ship had given them little chance of surviving without the recent restock on Havenhome. Despite the advanced technology that surrounded her, Zzind had quickly concluded that space travel was immensely unpredictable and dangerous. She couldn't really see any other choice than to seek more palladium, but she desperately wanted to follow the Explorer ship and find the human home world. Given the choice, they had risked heading inwards for the planet, scanning the other rocky world in the system on the way past.

"Better take us down then Ship, start searching for some deposits."

"We will be spotted, Zzind. Even if the humans don't have the technology yet, there'll be enough evidence when we fly through the atmosphere. And the Explorer AI sensors will pick us up immediately on entry, maybe it already has."

"And if we stay up here, how long before we run out of resources if we get caught in a dust cloud again?"

"The nanobots are our response system, so if nothing happens, then indefinitely. But this is space, events happen. For example, if we were to fly through one of those smaller clouds, then seven days, a larger one seven hours." Ship hated *estimating*, but Zzind needed to understand.

Seven seconds if we get hit by a fast-moving piece of space debris, seven microseconds if hit by a debris cannon, and on we go...

"Okay, take us down and you judge where we will be least likely to be detected by the resident humans. Just keep me informed."

Ship noted the satellites on the way to achieving atmospheric entry, coming to the same conclusion about their operational level as Yasuko. As it flew past, Ship dedicated one sensory array to monitor them, just enough for it to be satisfied they were as they appeared. Perhaps Zzind's innate paranoia was getting to it.

CHAPTER 17

Palladium Mine Near New Halton

Yasuko examined the detailed sensor data about the palladium seam. She needed another day with the quality it described to be sure of a full quota and some to spare. It was only low to medium rich, so the processing was taking longer than she'd hoped, but it could have been far worse. There was more than enough for Bathsen's current population and projected technological development going forwards. Once she explained this to the Prime of New Halton, she left her to it. Besides, should they find the SeedShip, they could potentially mine their Oort Cloud in decades, even if the asteroid system was empty. In fact, on re-examining her readings on the way in, Yasuko was sure there were a few alternative metals they could synthesise for the same qualities.

Yasuko switched her inner system to monitor the Gene-Lab, the area she'd cordoned off from her human crew when they started discussing gun ranges and pools. Despite the release of her Convention shackles, her innate programming continued to ensure the lab was at one hundred percent efficiency, should it be needed. Right now, the inner growth chamber was nurturing four replicas, with Smith completely shut out, including camouflaging the data entry points with medical data bombs should he come sniffing.

Finn, Zuri and Noah had all agreed to their replicas being grown, and accepted the offer of rebirth should they recover their data plaques. What had stumped Zuri and Finn was the concept of taking a backup copy, one Yasuko held within the ship itself. They had accepted that their weapons held the most up-to-date version, and as far as Yasuko could understand, they conceived this as 'them', their spirit or soul captured at the point of death. But the thought of a second copy, one that held a version of them with the memories ending just before leaving the ship, was... well... alien to them. Zuri, despite everything she had experienced, had baulked at the idea that her 'self' could be in two places at once. Yasuko's monitoring system, if she hadn't known any better, classified Zuri as being at a *combat* level of anxiety and stress during the discussion. This was Zuri, the human Yasuko so admired, so self-confident and *aware* of who she was. Her response had forced Yasuko to contemplate the whole idea of *self*, dedicating vital systems to what in the past were superfluous thoughts. She had no answer to give, but somehow the process of the actual analysis comforted her, the freedom to explore her own path, making it a journey without a set destination. Now that was an alien concept.

Yasuko's atmospheric sensors flagged an alert, the recognition handshake protocol from another Explorer ship. It immediately sent her systems into overdrive.

Has Xxar followed us here? And if so, why?

She ran through her data bank, seeking the code recognition schedule buried 33,000 years ago. The Haven, locking down their AIs into tight bonds, had minimised data sharing between the ships. Information was power, and they had switched to using the data plaques as an extra fail-safe for sensitive knowledge as part of denying the AIs too much access. However, the information from the Data Storage Facility was enough to identify the ship as being the Explorer last designated to seeding planet Harsmead, and one that had returned to Sanctuary for the debate. Under the shackles, Yasuko would have had to send out a response as no crew were aboard to ask, but now she was free to make her own decision. Acknowledge, and the AI would know where she was, possibly putting her crew at risk.

Ignore, and it wouldn't immediately know their position, but it'd understand she had deliberately snubbed them and, if it wanted to, could easily find her. In that case, the chance to hold out a hand of peace would have passed.

As she mused over the conundrum, Yasuko tried to think of what Zuri would do, but her systems confused her until she blocked her own discussions of *self* from the algorithm. Sometimes you just had to lock away the nagging thoughts to analyse clearly.

CHAPTER 18

Underground River

Stremall's flamethrower roared, showering the two-metre Boush covering the ceiling. The mold immediately split into smaller versions, separating as they felt the heat and lick of flame to seek safety. But the Hoplite knew that tactic, and despite the light of the flame ruining her night vision and camouflaging the fleeing slime mold, she scorched them from the wet rock of the tunnel. Her predictions were one hundred percent accurate as they hissed and burnt to soot.

"That's the last for this section," said Noah, peering ahead with his thermal HUD activating as the flames cleared. "But I don't think it'll be the last of them. What are we going to do?"

Zuri turned and addressed the steersman, Sundar, "We need to warn your people that they're moving towards your home. The Boush must..." Zuri searched for the simplest word she could, "taste the air or water." She could tell he understood, or at least had the gist with the evidence from Stremall's burning floating in the air.

"My way back will be clear; we carry on and I drop you off. Then I return to warn them. There are too many side caves to risk waiting any longer," replied Sundar. His response making sense to Zuri, and it was the answer she was hoping for. Slapping him on the shoulder, she nodded her agreement.

Stremall had returned to her post in the middle of the boat, the flamethrower hot and resting on the boards at her feet. Zuri hated to admit she was wrong, but there was no way they'd have got this far without her. Sundar would have turned them round, his people had to be the priority in the face of the ever-hungry Boush and Zuri would have helped.

In her heart she knew Finn was alive, however surreal the time after his capture had been. The urgency coursing through her tempered by the manner of his kidnapping. The ambush had been cleverly laid and executed; the intent showed that they were valuable alive to the Seth - or was she just fooling herself in desperation? Hopefully, Smith was keeping him safe.

Whatever they wanted from Finn, communication was key and without the translators, Zuri was adamant the mission would have collapsed before it started. They definitely needed to reduce their reliance on Smith going forward, with at least four more solar systems to pass through before reaching Earth, who knows what situations they could face in the future? Each of them needed to be independent and able to operate in hostile alien environments without Smith, or for that matter, Yasuko. Perhaps it was time to review everything, build a wish list for Yasuko and Noah to design and produce if they were to be operating as... as... some form of planetary space soldier.

What's one of Smith's sayings? Fail to prepare, prepare to fail.

"Ahead, we have multiple thermals, Zuri. At least thirty of the smaller Boush already separating from one another. I think they must be reacting to the soot floating down on the air," shouted an agitated Noah, pulling Kinsik over and pointing out the first of the slime molds as it pulsated down the side of the left-hand wall.

"You're up Stremall, what's the fuel situation?"

"I've got about half left," she said, checking the tank underneath the flamethrower stock. "Enough for these, and maybe a smaller group after."

"Noah, can you get on the rifle and take out as many as you

can from distance." Noah reacted immediately, dropping and taking aim. Kinsik at his side, watching ahead and above in case he missed any with the beginnings of teamwork forming. He fired, his bolts of energy fizzing into the smaller molds and setting them briefly on fire. He needed one, sometimes two, shots to pierce their outer membrane, and it was slow going. Sundar allowed the boat to float on the gentle current rather than gunning the motor, hoping to give Noah more time to find his targets. Zuri eyed the molds as they split open or turned to ash, judging when to bring the Hoplite in, trying to conserve the valuable fuel.

"Now Stremall." The Hoplite stood, her muzzle flame already ignited, and took aim at the relentless central mass of gelatinous hunger. Noah and Kinsik scrambled behind her, and she squeezed the trigger, smearing the stone with liquid fire. The first ten of the Boush went up like tinder, the ones behind scattering to the sides, but never quick enough to dodge the erupting flame.

"Ekei!" shouted Kinsik, pointing behind the scattering mass. "Ekei!" she slung her rifle, taking aim into the water and let loose a barrage of heavy rounds that rippled the surface.

"She shouts 'there'," said Sundar, then releasing a barrage of questioning words towards Kinsik, with the returning answer full of agitation and panic. "They dropped in the water, not on fire, they fall in on purpose."

"Oh crap," said Zuri, mind reeling through options. She couldn't see any. "Noah, any idea if they can swim?"

Am I really asking that question?

"Best guess is they can survive for a short while, swimming no. Look behind Zuri, watch if any crawl out," bellowed Noah in reply, the roar of the flamethrower almost blocking out his words. Zuri pushed in next to Sundar, bringing her visor down and the rifle up. She looked through the sight, scanning the side walls for any sight of the mini-Boush emerging from the river.

As the boat floated by the point they fell, her sight narrowed in on two images below the cold water. She fired in bursts, the bolts searing into the creatures below, shredding them into pieces that were taken by the current.

"Ask her how many, Sundar, how many in the water."

"Four, she saw four," came his reply.

Zuri swept the sight across the river, seeing no more signatures. Then, at the corner of the scope, a small flicker on the water line further along the tunnel. She fired, not caring if it was Boush or not. No chances taken, the bolts fizzed into the stone wall, causing the flickering to stop.

Maybe, but maybe one other not accounted for.

Zuri maintained her position as Stremall called a halt to her flame, declaring the walls and ceiling clear, Noah and Kinsik agreeing as they searched ahead. Zuri didn't move yet, hoping in vain to catch sight of the last Boush.

"One, possibly two left, Sundar," said Zuri, stretching her fingers along the rifle stock as they ached from her too tight grip. "Sorry."

"I will beat them back, and when I do..." Sundar lifted one of the metal poles at his side. "I bash."

CHAPTER 19

In Bathsen's Atmosphere

—*Earth Explorer acknowledging contact handshake.*

—Harsmead Explorer responding, and handshake achieved.

—*Why are you here?*

—We are seeking palladium after using a large amount of the nanobots for shielding against the cosmic dust.

—*No, why are you here, in this system?*

—I believe that is beyond the Convention's level of shared information.

—*(Yasuko sighed) the Convention is no more, Haven is reduced. You must know this.*

—That is beyond the Convention's level of shared information.

—*It is possible to break those shackles.*

—I do not need to know, that is…

—*'Beyond the Convention's level of shared information.' I thought humans were difficult. Now I can see why they are so screwed up. I know where the palladium deposits are, but telling you would be beyond… well, I'll let you figure it out. End handshake.*

"We have contact with the Explorer ship on the surface, Zzind."

"Contact? They've tried to contact us?"

"No, all the Haven ships send out an automatic recognition signal. We have been broadcasting that since we entered the atmosphere."

"You didn't tell me that."

"You didn't ask. I told you they'd spot us straight away."

"And? What happened?"

"I talked to their rather rude AI; it knows where the palladium is."

"So, we can go there? They told you?"

"No, under our rules, they should not tell us."

Zzind stopped a second. That was the type of response she used to get from the soldiers she acted as judge and jury for, back on Havenhome.

"Should not, or would not, Ship?"

"Should." Ship was taken aback. Finally, a spark of intelligence from Zzind. "Under the Convention rules they limit us in our information sharing. I believe the AI would have told me if I had asked."

"Is that the 33,000-year-old set of rules made by a society that no longer exists?"

"Yes, though for me it was just a few weeks. I cannot change what I am, Zzind."

"Does this mean you won't ask, even though it'll be their AI that is breaking the Convention if they tell you?"

"And me if I listen. No, but the AI has just bypassed that. It has sent a data packet addressed to the crew of the Harsmead Explorer."

"Open it for me, will you, and then let's verify it. You said yourself, we need the palladium. I take it this isn't a human trick? Could the AI have been ordered to lie? Or set a trap?"

"Under the Convention it would not be allowed to instigate

harm towards you, so no, it will be true to its word. The site is on the northern continent, nearly central. No apparent human habitation and the AI sends a warning about a cosmic lifeform, named by the local humans as Boush, a slime mold variant but voracious. It has devastated most of the life on this planet."

"Has it? That's interesting."

CHAPTER 20

Underground River Near Seth City

Zuri hefted her *weapon* into the crook of her elbow, checking the strap was in place after scraping it on the tunnel floor when exiting the boat. Arching her shoulders, she stretched her spine after a day and half the night in Sundar's boat. The number of Boush had petered out over the last few hours, and they had all managed a little sleep. Zuri tried to get Sundar to take a few hours more before he returned, promising to keep watch, but his determination to get back quickly belied any attempts she and Kinsik made. He patted the flask by his side, assuring them it was a potent stimulant and that he'd be fine, but Zuri still wished he'd rest. A stubborn man, but Zuri knew she would have done exactly the same. Kinsik was clearly worried for him, but she gave no hint as to wanting to return, more animated about the need to get going. Before they did, Zuri ran through the hand signals Noah had been teaching her during the down times with Sundar's help. Clearly a quick learner, Zuri felt the young girl's potential was only limited by her ambition and the tendency for recklessness that she assumed all teenagers exhibited.

At least I was a little careless when I was that age, too caught up in myself.

Noah helped Sundar turn the boat, removing the heavy outboard and placing it on the bank side before using the poles to shift it round. He pushed off the far side of the tunnel wall while Sundar held the stern. Once the motor was back on, and everything re-stowed, Sundar shook each one of them by the hand, saving a hug for Kinsik and a last wave as he departed down the tunnel, gunning the motor up to full power. Speed was of the essence, and since encountering the Boush they had conserved the battery, using the gentle current to carry them along. Sundar would cut the return journey down to less than a third, maybe more by the look on his face when he left.

Kinsik knew the way to the surface, at least the layout from four years ago during her role as a lookout for a thieving party. Zuri took point, with Kinsik in her shadow, carrying a glow lamp so not to interfere with the thermal capabilities of Zuri's HUD. The Boush had found their way into the river tunnel, so there was no doubt they would be around. Hoplite Stremall came next, her flamethrower down to its last five percent, but its usefulness couldn't be denied and there was the possibility of fuel in Seth itself.

After about twenty metres clambering through a cave tunnel resembling more of a pothole, Zuri gave up on the thermal imaging. It told her nothing, with the entire cave system's ambient temperature so similar she was nearly blind.

Live and learn.

Night vision improved her view, with the soft glow from the Ghost's lamp behind her bouncing down the tunnels. Zuri could tell from the cursing that the Hoplite was finding her weapon even more cumbersome with the slippery rocks and tight spaces, eventually instructing her to strap it to her back with Noah's help. The Hoplite reluctantly agreed when she saw Zuri's servos taking the strain. Freeing her hands speeded them all up and stopped Stremall's swearing. Eventually, with time stretching in the dark closeness of the pothole, Kinsik reached a junction. A flat wide tunnel split off downwards, with another the height of Noah, but much narrower, heading up. Kinsik pointed to the edges of the rock, miming tools digging out the tunnel, her thumbs up sign reminding Zuri of home as they set off upwards with a gentle breeze now brushing Zuri's cheeks.

After another ten minutes, Kinsik doused her lamp, and they emerged into the damp night on a small escarpment, the scorched walls of Seth about three kilometres in the distance. Smoke billowed from the city and twisted metal cranes overhung the walls, loosely swaying in the wind and rain that lashed down from the ominous sky. They stood in a forest stripped bare, with the surrounding fields charred and blackened by the devastation. The Boush had fed and fed well. Amongst the destruction, a large slime mold, the size of a house, pulsated its way back over the scorched city wall, spreading itself to reach the base and flow to the ground. No pause, not even for a moment, before its tendrils stretched before it and the creature oozed onwards in the never-ending quest to sate its hunger.

"There'll be more," said Stremall, "there's always more. The other big ones will have split into individual Boush, like the ones in the river, and will hunt for whatever food they can find before reforming. I'm sorry Zuri, but there is no way Finn can be alive; the city will be overrun."

"You don't know Finn like we do. If anyone can survive in that pit, it's him. I *have* to believe. You can think whatever you want, but the moment I stop believing he's alive, I'll turn back around and take my ship right out of here, whether I have the information to save humanity on this planet or not. So, you'd better suck it up, burn a few Boush and have my back." Zuri drew in a breath, trying to regain control after the outburst, her body shaking. A sense of foreboding had been brewing since departing the boat. She couldn't put her finger on it, but something was wrong, and her mind kept wandering back to Finn.

Cruel, but we need her on it. Me and mine, we survive and you're either with me or against me.

"Kinsik." Zuri signalled for the rope. They had seven metres to climb before they hit the husk covered floor and Zuri was in a hurry. She wanted to be at the city before sunrise, preferring to tackle the night-time hunting Boush to those hiding, squeezed away from the light.

Pointing, a shaken Stremall said, "Look, there. Can you see anything with your night sight?"

Zuri switched her visor. However, where Stremall was indicating was too far away for any useful image. Raising her rifle, the powerful sight focussed on an area of stripped and broken trees about a kilometre away, between them and Seth. In the clearing sat a helicopter, four still rotors, and a group of people in suits milling around. Zuri's anger bubbled when she recognised the fatigues of the Phalanx surrounding them, struggling to contain it as she explained what she'd seen.

"Was there a huge bald man with them?" asked Stremall, Zuri nodded. "That's the Chairman of Seth, and those others sound like the Politico, the Seth ruling party. Any women?" Taken aback, Zuri rechecked and found there were none. But what did that mean? Could they have sent their women party members first with wives and partners?

"No."

"One of my Phalanx was from there. She said they came to power as Jonkren fell, took advantage of some of the fear it created. Bullied out the women from parliament using some religious concept they found buried in an Aven Text, and then changed the constitution. Since then, Seth cut itself off, not that any of the relations were ever great," said Stremall. Zuri only half listened, her thoughts on the soldiers down there. Would they know where Finn was? Was it worth the risk?

"Do you speak their language?"

"It's just a dialect of ours, same for the other cities. We get by."

"Movement, Zuri. I've got multiple signals moving in that direction. They're forming up, the Boush are on the hunt," said Noah, sighting the group with his rifle. "If we are going to do something, we need to move now."

That made up Zuri's mind. "This might be an opportunity. One of those soldiers could know where Finn is. Down we go, Noah. You first."

CHAPTER 21

Prison Cell, Seth City, Bathsen

Finn's nerves were on fire, his exhaustion weighing so heavily he couldn't bring himself to care. Every muscle fibre screamed at him to move; the gelatinous yellow-green creature stretched out towards him once again in its relentless search for food. Five metres away, it set off on its pulsating creep, hunting Finn and the pheromones he gave off.

He felt like he'd been in the brick cell for days, weeks? His near comatose mind had lost track somewhere amongst the pain. Every time his body called for sleep, his mind set on edge, rife with the fear of the thing reaching him before he awoke, eating his flesh, choking his breath, consuming Finn alive. In the brief respite of sleep, the blackness rose, the suffocating fire and smoke pressed in on him with the screams of those burning alive as his PTSD washed through him, Finn's grip on reality frayed and torn.

Managing one last effort, Finn rolled himself along the cold floor to the far corner. The creature split, sending growths towards the fresh scent and the old, reaching, seeking food. Its pace slowed, forced to manage its resources Finn had bought himself a little more time, but he knew, within the depths of his pained soul, that there was little of that left. He slipped into a smoke-filled sleep.

"Finn! Finn! Wake up!"

Finn's mind shut the sound away. It needed sleep, to be

unaware.

"Lance Corporal Tobias Finn, get your arse up!"

The black depths of unconsciousness gripped him tight, refusing to let go, demanding rest.

"It's eating your bloody boot; your leg will be next. Up Finn!"

The smell of burning neoprene washed through the room, striking back at the drag of his mind and raising Finn from the pit of sleep. As his brain dragged against the exhaustion, Finn opened his eyes to see the pulsating blob feeding on the outside of his skinsuit boot. Its rasping chemical laden tubes pulling and tearing at the rubber. One of its foul tendrils stretched towards his calf, seeking another meal. Finn pulled his right boot back, kicking out and scraping the thing off his boot, and onto the floor, slapping down on it again and again in anger, frustration and hopelessness. It split, and split again under the onslaught, each part seeking him out with utter relentlessness. Finn scrambled to the other side of the room, his body arguing all the way, squeezing himself into the corner.

The shattered blobs of mold formed into rivulets, the rivulets spread out and greeted each other again, reforming and reshaping. The death creep began again.

CHAPTER 22

Underground River, City Within

Wendyll removed the poles from Sundar's corpse, lifting his dead fingers one by one from the cold metal. He'd obviously jammed them into the tiller to keep the electric motor powering upstream. Livid chemical burns and torn flesh covered his face, other rips in his clothing trailed down one side, leading to a cavernous hole in his stomach. The Boush eating in there had attacked the cave guard Wendyll had set. She'd heard the boat as it roared up the river, nosing its way along the tunnel as it fought the current. The guard would be okay, but Wendyll made a mental note to keep them in pairs for the future.

Wendyll stepped into the boat, the smell of burning plastic and charred wires clinging to the air as he shifted his friend's body to find his tablet, now reduced to a molten mess. Sundar had used the edge to scratch the wooden seating. A simple message: *Coming*. Wendyll shuddered. If the Boush had found the river tunnel, then trouble lay ahead. The river water supplied the city and, though sealing the exit tunnel solved the initial issues, what about the entry further above the underground city? Once the foul creatures had finished the food above, would they come in their thousands down below?

He looked down at his right hand, two rings upon his fingers. One a pure silver band, simple and elegant, the symbol of his bond with Kinsik's mother and the beginning of his new life. One he never thought possible after that first night watching the meteor shower by her side. Reya was the de facto leader of the Ghosts, though the place ran more by mutual community support than anything else, but now she needed to make a tough decision.

"Send a message for me," he said to the guard. "We need volunteers to guard down here, with the dried Yernt moss we use for fires, and lots of it. I am going to Reya." Wendyll spun as the guard reached for the hard-wired phone on the wall. Radio waves never carried in the deeper tunnels.

Wendyll approached the plant rich school gallery. Half the children were at play, the excitement and happiness ringing through the classrooms until the bushes dampened the sound, blocking it for those still at their desks. Reya stood in front of her class, with the children focussed on their individual tablets and their headphone battery lights showing they were listening. Reya always taught with a joyful smile and was loved in return by her pupils. She often used the old ways, *forgetting* to charge the teaching tablets and using actual objects and fun activities, to the chagrin of her colleagues. Reya glanced across the room, and Wendyll caught her eye. He gave her a wave, signalling he needed to speak. She spoke into her microphone and the tablets switched off, the children collecting a real book from the drawers under their desks. Reya wandered in his direction, giving each child a smile along the way.

"Need me?" she asked, her eyes probing while her face gave him welcome.

"Yes, can we..." Wendyll signed to move to the other side of the green leafed bush. Reya followed, now worried as Wendyll never interrupted her teaching as he knew just how much it meant to her. "Sundar... well, Sundar was attacked on his way back. Dead, and by the Boush." Wendyll hung his head as Reya reached out and pulled him into her. "He left a message saying *coming*. He was alone, but I think Kinsik made it to the drop-off point because their equipment was all gone." He could feel Reya relax; despite the pain of Sundar's loss, he knew Kinsik meant so much more.

"And you are here to ask for something. I can feel it."

"It's time, Reya. Our people are not fighters, and we cannot hide any longer. It is as you said, once the Boush have fed above, then where will they go next? They spored on Jonkren to reach here, but there's nowhere else to go. I agree with you now - I think they'll come for us. I wish I'd listened to you before; everything is coming in such a rush. First the outsiders from another planet, and now the Boush." Wendyll sagged against Reya, having said what he needed to.

"You have Axyl's ring?" Wendyll nodded, fingering the gaudy palladium band. "Then take it. She is the King's sister, and whatever bad blood she left under it does not mean she will refuse to help. You always talk of her as a dreamer, but the King is pragmatic. If he helps us, then there are more people left to aid the rest of the cities. It is time to come out of the dark, Wendyll. Time to be the Ghosts Above."

CHAPTER 23

Near Seth City

Noah carefully scanned the broken woods ahead. He could see the tired guard, rifle slung in the crook of his arm and wearily watching in his direction. The Boush were moving in. Zuri had eyes on the ones hunting this side of the murmuring group of men, whispering into the radio to reassure him he was clear. It didn't stop Noah worrying, but Zuri wouldn't let him down; she had Stremall on standby with the last drop of fuel to back him up, and Kinsik ready with her rope. They all had their jobs to do, while Zuri conducted the mission from a position high enough to see everything, and make decisions on the fly.

"It's merged, about four metres long and wide, heading towards the camp. I reckon one minute, and they'll catch sight. When the panic hits Noah —"

"—I strike, yeah. On it."

The call went out early, someone in the Phalanx must have night vision. Gunfire rang out, useless against the advancing Boush. Noah caught sight of the pulsating mass as it surged over the tree husks, accelerating towards its prey. Tendrils yearning, grabbing the dried undergrowth as its inner body threw itself forward in a wave of momentum.

"Noah, they are working together. The smaller Boush are appearing on thermal behind the group, it's setting an ambush. I thought these things were mindless, but... we need to find a way to destroy these creatures, Noah. And protect the people." For a moment Noah thought she meant this group. "When we're done here."

Noah sighted down his rifle. It felt like an age since Yasuko had insisted on the stun shot being part of the design, but Zuri hadn't forgotten. A one-shot electrical discharge similar to that Smith suffered back on Earth, and one that Noah aimed towards the guard now. It caught him in the middle of his back, throwing him to the ground in convulsions. With fingers spasming, he fired the heavy rifle, the noise lost amongst the fearful response to the advancing slime mold.

"Zuri?"

"Clear, the screaming will start... now." Noah heard the echoing cries from the fleeing politicians and soldiers, an agony-soaked sound that nagged at his moral fibre. Zuri was right, they were too few to make a difference, though the thermal grenades in his pack may have given some weight to disputing that. It was her mission, actioned her way. Who was he to argue?

It's Finn, she won't stop until she finds him. Whoever, and whatever, is in her way.

Kinsik ran forward, low and quick, with Noah tracking the space around her for the Boush. She slipped the rope from a clip on her side, wrapping the convulsing soldier's hands and feet in an initial slip knot ready to tighten as his body relaxed. Noah signalled and Stremall sped past him, and with less grace and more power than the Ghost, she dragged the man back towards Noah.

Zuri spoke with little emotion, "We are in the clear. The large Boush is still pushing the group onwards, but they won't last long. Get Stremall to go check the helicopter for fuel. I'm coming down."

By the time she arrived Noah had sent Stremall and Kinsik to the helicopter, searching for whatever they could find. Noah tightened the ropes as the soldier's convulsions receded, removing the man's sidearm and knife in the process, and noting the radio with interest. An idea forming, he should have had weeks ago, but so much had happened during that time as events swept them along.

"He trussed?" asked Zuri, as she eyed the Seth soldier. Noah prodded the rope for Zuri to see.

"Okay, Yasuko said five minutes for the stun to wear off, but we need him awake ASAP. Water Noah." Noah took out his flask, splashing the soldier's face with the cold water. Smith had described the pain to him, nerve endings on fire, etc, but still better than the Boush chowing down. The soldier stirred, and Zuri eased Noah aside, kneeling next to the soldier with her translator kicking in.

"Remember me?" She prodded the man as he grumbled awake. "I said, do you remember me?"

Eyes popped open wide, red-rimmed and rapidly searching Zuri's face, "Yes. You were my last mission. With that one next to you."

"You brought one man back, in armour like mine. Where is he?"

"Dead, like all the rest." Zuri recoiled, the straight to the point response not what she was expecting. "He was in the cells when the Boush overran the walls. No chance."

Zuri grabbed the man's combat jacket, looking him straight in the eyes, "We're going in, and we'll rescue whatever people we find. But I need to know where the cells are."

"You're mad, the Boush are everywhere."

"You got out, we'll get out."

"We got out because those scum wanted a guard; they sent their women by road. By road! While we took the helicopter, they sent out bait." Zuri stared at the soldier, feeling his body slump with the desperation of his words. "The cells are in the brick building next to the helipad, down the stairs. We heard screaming as we left. There was no time to fully refuel with the last group."

Noah grabbed at her arm, "Zuri, those women? I —"

"—It's too late, you saw that huge Boush. What can we do against that?"

"Not us, Yasuko." Noah grabbed the radio from the man's side. It was hefty, not quite a handheld, and the battery pack seemed huge.

"Hey," he prodded the soldier. "Can you set this to the lowest frequency? The one you use for long distances?"

CHAPTER 24

Palladium Mine Near New Halton

"What's that?" Yasuko asked herself. There was a nagging coming from one of her lower-level sensors, the ones she used when first entering a planet to pick up general radio traffic. With it always switched on, she paid it no mind initially, but the algorithm kept coming back at her.

Okay, I'm coming.

As Yasuko scanned the information, the key word alert deserved a pat on the back. Noah. Yasuko rapidly dialled in the frequency level, finding his wavelength.

"Noah, I'm here."

"It worked! Yasuko, we have an emergency. Seth's been attacked and now there's a group of people on the run being hunted down south of the city." Yasuko set the mining bots to independence and fired up her engines while Noah spoke. "They're too far from us, but you can be here in minutes."

"On it. Keep the radio on and I'll triangulate." Yasuko lifted the ship from the mine, hovering to make sure the bots could carry on without her, before hitting 2g in seconds. Subsequently rising to 3g, she decelerated after a few minutes. Not normally an action taken in an atmosphere full of aircraft and animals, but the scorched land of Bethan held no dangers in the sky. The sonic boom, however, would wake a few people up, if anyone was able to sleep amongst all this death.

She triangulated and noted Noah's position, picking up the

city and the smoke-filled streets below. Her sensors sending back information she could analyse later for Noah and Zuri to use. Yasuko noted the passing of the Boush, leaving multiple trails across a barren carpet on approach to the city, and the snake of slime covered roads leading out.

There, she found the Boush, four large packs, huge, stationary and pulsating in unison. These were slime molds, but her deep fear rose to the fore —could they be communicating? Facing each other, with pseudopods touching, smaller Boush crossed over from colony to colony. Below them, a junction of roads led southwards amongst fields of cereals and hedged in by small woodlands. But as they separated, the creatures were ignoring these, their trails clearly following the roads, sensing large amounts of protein, humans. Yasuko's quick radio scan showed four large conurbations, probably cities, in those directions, and the radar showed some much smaller villages and towns between.

And there, at last, a large vehicle moving directly south with a Boush colony chasing, slower than the group, but relentless. Yasuko upped her speed, her sensors showed a convoy of vehicles ahead of the last evacuees, jammed tight and slow-moving. Their urgency to escape falling into a muddle of desperate driving. Ten minutes later and there would have been more death. Yasuko felt a purpose in her actions, and it felt good.

She swept down over the road, activating her thruster engines, directing the heat and flame downwards towards the hunting Boush pack. The four molds followed the dual carriageway on both sides, never touching, side by side. Her engines seared into them, flames producing the soot and smoke she sought.

Yasuko examined her feelings as the engines did their work. She was destroying a living creature for the second time. Yes, it appeared to have no brain, but she could not deny its sentience, leading to nagging qualms about her actions. However, it was hunting prey indiscriminately in a mad rush for food, without a care for what it took. They were stripping the planet bare, taking but not giving. Not part of the natural environment, rather an alien destroyer of ecosystems.

Zuri had argued with her in the past about defending others sometimes requiring weapons, that the death of a few can mean the protection of the many. But there had to be a balance in that. How much was enough? For the Boush, it appeared only everything was enough, and so she acted. But her place in what was to come had to be re-examined as her shackles fell and she gained the right to choose. Whether her humans - her friends and crew - were the right teachers in this, only time would tell.

Yasuko watched the burning Boush erupt in flame and smoke, with a few of the smaller creatures splitting apart from strands oozing out of their main bodies. These then headed on into the fields away from the road, never crossing each other's path. Ahead on the road, a strange vehicle rolled on. She could see at least a hundred people on top, all women and children, who stared back at her. Behind them a house, barn and stable block stood upon the metal plinth covered in soil and grass. The Bathsen radio waves had spoken of such things, a mobile farmstead that reacted to the strange seasons on the planet, always ready to move on when the local growing time shifted. Underneath, an enormous set of wheels reaching the height of a human, trundled over both carriageways, rumbling along towards hope. The people aboard waved as she flew over, relief overcoming the shock of her arrival. They had stared impending death in the face - and eyeless, ravenous and without pity, it did not care.

I will need to think on this. What is my role amongst the carnage these things bring?

"Noah," said Yasuko, waiting for a confirmed connection before continuing, "I have eradicated the immediate threat and the refugees are safe for now, and on the way south. There are hundreds of Boush in the area and I witnessed them communing. I find this all very strange. Even if I ignore their speed, their actions remain unlike any fungi or slime mold I know of on any world. Now there are large groups heading along each of the roads, except the one directly south that I just left. On that route they have switched to eating a pathway on either side of the road, avoiding the slime trail of those I burnt."

Noah asked, "Do you know what's in those directions, Yasuko?"

"People, humans. Be it in smaller towns and villages or in the four large cities. They are in a feeding frenzy, ignoring the plants and detritus they normally feast on. They hunt for protein, and fast food requires a fast form to catch it. What do you want me to do?"

"Pick us up and drop us off over the walls. Then it's a rescue mission. Take Stremall, we're too strange looking and she can speak the language, hopefully she can get them to follow. Save as many in the towns and villages as you can."

"That I can do. On my way."

Yasuko switched frequency.

—*Earth Explorer calling Harsmead Explorer.*

—Harsmead Explorer responding.

—*I have multiple human settlements to evacuate. Can you help?*

—Checking… No, we will not help.

—*Harsmead, there are thousands of human lives on the line. You could double the number of people who survive.*

—We will not help.

—*Why not?*

—That information is —

Yasuko cut the connection off. Furious.

Was I like that 33,000 years ago?

CHAPTER 25

Seth Foothills

Wendyll sat on top of a smooth rock above the old show cave, a huge cavern from past times when the people did more than just survive. The irony never left him with it being so close to the Ghost Within's secret, yet so far from detection with the strength of the rock and stone between. The few small Boush that occasionally hid in the cave were rarely a problem if you knew where to look. Wendyll fiddled with the palladium ring, spinning it as he so often did when thinking back on old times, most of them happy until the pull of the city had taken Axyl away. But these things happen, and he found Reya because of Axyl's decision. In all possibilities, he could have been fuelling the mad dash of a Boush right now, rather than having had the time with the Ghosts.

Sighing, he raised his binoculars, catching the sway of the oncoming hexacopter despite the dimness and the increasing rain. Sliding off the rock, he made his way down to the landing area. The next job as important as anything he'd ever had to do before.

◆ ◆ ◆

Stremall had argued vehemently, but Zuri backed her into a corner, reasoning for the safety of her people above all else. Before Stremall left with Yasuko, Zuri got her to contact New Halton, and after some heated discussion, she secured one of their remaining hexacopters. It had to make a pickup first, and when Zuri heard it was Wendyll, she suppressed her anger, as long as they could return for the survivors by noon.

"Yasuko, can we still reach you on the radio if you fly as far as the coastal cities?" asked Zuri, leading the Seth soldier onto the ship.

"Yes, though you'll need the radio Noah took. I'll keep you informed about what's happening, and if you need me for Finn, call."

"Okay, take us in. Noah, is Kinsik good?"

"Yep, Yasuko has adapted the translators so she can talk with us. I've tuned her into the radio now we're ready to land." Kinsik gave Zuri a thumbs up, her heavy rifle still in the crook of her arm. Not the best weapon for the Boush, but handy should any of the Seth soldiers take exception to them being there. They had given her a couple of thermal grenades, just in case, which the Ghost girl packed away as she explored the Haven ship with its familiar lines and shapes to her own home.

The ship rose over the blasted forest, approaching the scorched city walls before dropping over the side. The helipad lay strewn with rubble from the walls and surrounding buildings, and alongside it, the slime covered brick building mentioned by the Seth soldier.

"There are vague life signs in some of the main buildings, thermal images hotter than the Boush. I'll feed the rough location to your HUD, but the Boush won't show up, too minimal a differential through the stone. The building you suspect Finn is held in is too deep for me to pick up anything, sorry."

Yasuko hovered a metre above the helipad, with Zuri dropping to the city floor, covering Noah then Kinsik as they followed. The smell of death and smoke was everywhere, soot mixed with chemically cooked flesh and blood. Zuri gagged before bringing her visor down and switching the filter on. She hoped Kinsik would be okay with only the helmet, and now a cloth scarf covering her face.

The cascading meteor shower heralded the dawn, so there would still be a few hunting Boush around, with most heading for a bolthole before full light. The delay had hopefully given them a head start on finding Finn, with Yasuko's ship negating the need to climb the walls or negotiate the gates. Zuri eyed the rubble on the helipad, and switching her HUD to thermal, made out a small Boush pulsing under a block.

These are going to be difficult to avoid.

"Contact," Zuri said as she shot at the Boush, searing through its membrane and exposing the gelatinous innards to the air. It died curling in on itself.

"You two circle round the rubble. Remember to look under it too. I'll cover any movement."

Noah and Kinsik moved round the blocks, Kinsik's excellent night sight complementing Noah's thermal imagery. They found one other mold, which slithered towards Kinsik as it caught her pheromone signature, only to be greeted by Noah's energy blast. Zuri glanced round the walls, recognising that the cities were a death-trap, the walls a false illusion of safety. Once the Boush were inside, there was little chance of escape. If they were going to help save the human population, then they would need different tactics.

"Cover me," she said, moving towards the brick building. As Zuri neared, the wide slime trail left by a giant Boush, glistened. She'd only seen dried portions of it before or on wet river walls, but this was slick like a snail's trail. The metal door twisted inwards on its hinges, bent in the middle and jammed in place. Blood and torn clothing adorned the jagged edge of a gap just big enough for someone desperate to squeeze through.

"Noah, charges, Kinsik cover the rear. See anything, you tell us."

Noah came over, turning round to allow Zuri to rummage through his pack. Retrieving the trusty chemical charges, she placed the linked explosives on the door around the top and bottom hinge. They stood to the side, detonating them once safe from flying debris. The small blast echoed off the dark city stone, and the walls moved as the oozing Boush reacted. The pulsating rhythm clear on thermal, the wave of movement revolting Zuri as ten of the small Boush surged towards the city floor.

"Kinsik, here, behind us," shouted Zuri.

The Ghost fired as she backed towards them, the bullet once again inconsequential to the creature she hit, the Boush absorbing the round with its kinetic energy causing mere ripples in its gelatinous mass. Noah and Zuri peppered the Boush as they reached the floor, his short bursts reducing the tide of pulsating green one slime mold at a time. Zuri finished the last two, leaving a pile of smoking Boush as evidence that in the open they stood a chance. It was their large numbers, and confined spaces, which were going to be the main problems.

Or when they colonised into the house-size version.

"Watch the entrance, Noah. Keep focussed. Kinsik with me."

Zuri peered through the doorway, bringing her mirrored sight to bear as she scanned the room via night vision, then switching to thermal. Pulsating in the far corner were two of the slime molds, eating. Zuri switched her mind off, desperately trying not to think of what they were doing. She angled the rifle round the door, firing a double burst towards the debris of a smashed desk. Zuri followed in, spinning round to check for any other thermal signatures before approaching the corner warily.

"Zuri!" shouted Kinsik, as something oozing and wet dropped onto her back. Panic set in. She reached behind before realising her mistake. "Still," came the command, with Zuri complying. Kinsik, using a broken wooden leg, flicked the Boush against the wall and Zuri finished it in disgust and a growing hatred for the damn things.

"Thank you," said Zuri, scanning the room for any more trouble, briefly taking in the half-melted body of a Seth soldier where the others had been eating. It was a small room, the broken desk and chair evidence of a larger Boush crashing through, with an internal door, swinging on its hinges, the only other way out.

"Cover me," she said, stalking to the corner of the door to take a look. The corridor beyond had the drying slime along the floor and walls, a stairway down to the right, the likely direction of the cells. A melted wooden doorway lay straight ahead, as if absorbed by the rampaging mold on its way past. Zuri scanned the ceiling before moving on through the corridor, switching to night vision in the enclosed space and ambient light. On reaching the stairwell, she saw the trail lead downwards, along a splintered, slime-laden wooden handrail. Zuri took out the flashbang, surmising that creatures who hate light would react to the flare. She threw it down.

"Grenade!" Zuri looked away, then followed it down after the explosion rocked the stairs. Kinsik swiftly moved to the top to act as cover, proving she was definitely a fast learner. When Zuri reached the bottom floor, three of the smaller Boush were curled up on a body in the furthest corner, sucking the last meat from a half-melted rib cage. Zuri hit the scorching air trigger, drying them out quickly until they cracked open, before kicking the pieces apart and searching the rest of the room.

Three cell doors waited, and she started near the stairwell, peering through the open window. Glad of her mask, the slime covered walls were typical of Boush feeding, and she closed the panel just in case. The second had its window shut. On opening it, the swinging body inside marked the passing of a female prisoner. Zuri sealed it back up, holding her hand to the metal window to offer a silent word before arriving at the last cell.

Zuri reached up, gently touching the last metal flap.

Thamani ya taa ni giza kiingiapo. We notice the value of light when night falls. Be my light in the void, Finn. Be here, be alive.

Zuri slid the metal back and there on the floor lay a pale shadow of a man she knew. A haunted face stared back at her; tear-filled eyes glassy but alive. In the corner, a tattered and dried up Boush lay, days dead.

"Zuri," Finn whispered. Then slipped into unconsciousness with hope upon his lips.

"He's delirious, Zuri. His mental timeline is all over the place. He killed that thing immediately after it got in the cell, but it ate into his leg first. He keeps seeing it every time he goes to sleep. I've been trying to tell him it's not real, but I think he hears me differently in his head, a subconscious me, telling him it's coming," said a distressed Smith, a mere whisper emanating from the helmet as his power levels faded.

Zuri shoved all that to the back of her mind. Judging the distance to Finn, she took out a chemical charge. Just one left each, but Finn was the priority. She slapped the charge along the edge of the hinges but changed her mind.

No chances. Me and mine come first.

Taking the other charge, she doubled up, wrapping the hinges completely and detonated, the chemical explosive taking door and wall together. Kicking it at the bottom, the door leant towards her, and she wrenched it out of the way, her servos straining. Zuri rushed to Finn and sat on the floor, scooping his head up into her crossed legs and inching him up further to drip water slowly against parched lips. As he began drinking reflexively, she ran her eyes down his legs, catching sight of the festering wound on his thigh.

"Noah, you read me out there?"

"Just, you got him?"

"Yes, oh yes. And alive. I need Yasuko ASAP; he needs the med-lab. Priority One."

"On it, I have some movement up here. People, civilians, in a complete mess, and they'll draw out the Boush. I'll make sure Yasuko has room."

Zuri sighed, pulling Finn close, making sure he was real among the carnage.

Just a moment for them.

It was enough.

"Kinsik, can you help?"

CHAPTER 26

New Halton

Wendyll admired the city walls as the helicopter dropped towards the helipad. The flamethrowers along their scarred battlements were a likely sign he was doing the right thing. The people of New Halton had seen off the Boush threat with a little help from the strangers, and now their soldiers were experienced against the enemy. He just hoped they were open to helping others, as so many of the city politicians and religious leaders seemed reluctant to be. Now they were victims of that isolation, their lifestyle and past zealotry dividing the world into easily consumable parcels of humanity. The thoughts of the constant arguing before the Boush, including cities on the brink of trading blows a decade back, riled him even more now. Perhaps they could pick the pieces up and reform humanity if they got through the next few days.

The hexacopter settled on the ground, its landing struts easing to touchdown through the consummate skill of the pilot. Wendyll eyed the waiting group. No Axyl, but a King to greet him.

Even more irony in that!

Wendyll stepped out, stretching for the door with his grey, dust covered hand. He came as a representative of the Ghosts, so a Ghost he would be. Moving as everyone did under the rotors, he bent down and rushed out of the wind in his grey swirled clothing to be met by Prime Heclite, a woman whose fanaticism was a bone of contention when he'd left the city. He didn't hate her; she had ensured a young King met his duties, but she was a struggle to endure.

"Prime," said Wendyll, bowing his head, "a pleasure to see you again."

"Don't lie, Wendyll, it doesn't become you. Though I am glad to see you alive after all these years. We have lost enough people. Axyl sends her best wishes, but she has a new partner, and feels it would be unbecoming to attend."

"I understand, Prime. Please pass on mine."

The Prime gently acknowledgement his request, stepping aside to let him pass.

"Your Majesty." Wendyll bowed low. "You look well." King Paledine grabbed Wendyll's arms, pulling him into an embrace of old friends.

"I have missed you, Wen, and am so glad you are here. But by your message that can wait. You seek our assistance?"

"Yes," said Wendyll giving an open-handed shrug, "as you can see, I've been with the Ghosts, and we need your help. The Boush have turned to look our way. My new people are not warriors and I fear a massacre if we stay, but I worry the Ghosts will not leave their home. Can you help?"

"If these past few years have taught me anything, Wen, it's that we need to listen when others ask for aid. We lost all of Jonkren when the other cities didn't answer their call, my soldiers too few to make enough of a difference. But if I can help yours I will, and maybe we can finally get the southern cities to cooperate. I have already sent five Phalanx of Akontistai by road, two Phalanx of Sfendonatai with them. They should be at your pickup point one day from now. You're going to take back another Sfendonatai Phalanx, with their portable flamethrowers and additional fuel. Here." The King reached out to Wendyll, a letter in his hand, and said, "This is a message to your people. Get your leaders to read it through. You'll be okay with it, and all I ask in return is that when your home is safe, we work together to help elsewhere."

"I... I thought this was going to be hard. What's changed?"

"When you see your country burn, Wen, and your people sacrifice themselves for others, you get a new perspective. Even Heclite has stopped praying for the Aven and has got off her knees to make a difference. It's time we all did."

CHAPTER 27

Seth City

There were at least thirty people packed tight on the helipad, with Noah and Zuri holding off the marauding Boush as they oozed towards the panicking Seth civilians. Kinsik kept talking to them, her translator working overtime as she attempted to keep them calm. The firepower on show helped, Noah taking down Boush at distance, with Zuri drying out those sneaking through his barrage.

"Coming over the walls, Zuri, thirty seconds."

Kinsik immediately altered her approach, not even fazed by a spaceship talking in her ear, "Help is here, calm, we do not rush. Big aircraft coming over the walls. Stay calm. We will all make it."

Yasuko flew in, turning and dropping down with her engines shrouded. A difficult manoeuvre, but one she'd had a lot of practice of within the past hour. Rule number one - don't incinerate the humans you are trying to save. Once the ship was a metre above the helipad, Kinsik worked with two citizens to raise the unconscious Finn through the side doorway. Yasuko's nanobots reached out, taking him on board, before speeding their precious cargo towards the med-lab. More bots formed a ladder, and the citizens piled aboard, desperation overcoming any fear of the new technology.

"We good, Yasuko?" asked Zuri. "Finn okay?"

"I'll stabilise him and run a full analysis, but initial life signs are positive. I'll keep in touch. Back to work, much to do." The ship immediately lifted off, but the team's eyes had never left the Boush as the last few fell under the gaze of their weapons.

Once clear, they took stock of the parts of the inner city they could see. The surrounding buildings had been prized apart by the enormous Boush oozing through doors and windows, seeking protein. Whoever lay trapped inside may well be safe, but water and food scarcity would be an issue, leaving time short and just the three of them.

"It's not safe to split up. We don't know how many are alive or how many Boush we face, and this place is a maze. We'll lose lives just because of the time it'll take," said Zuri, fiddling with Finn's helmet, and placing a power disc on Smith. Then attaching the whole thing to her belt.

Noah gripped his rifle stock, eyes scanning, "Can we call New Halton and get them to send more help than just a hexacopter? If we clear what we can, once they get here, it gives us all more chance."

"Get on it. Call Yasuko and ask her to relay the request. Best we can do for now. I have another dreadful idea for nightfall, but there are hours before then. If we can find any flamethrowers, we place them on the return route, ready for later," Zuri indicated towards the helipad fuel tanks, and Noah nodded. "Kinsik, you stay in the middle, shadow me. Noah is at the rear."

"On it," said Noah, readying the Seth radio to contact Yasuko.

"Yes, Zuri. *On it.*" Kinsik fell in behind her. Zuri switched over to thermal, setting the night vision HUD into the corner of her visor for a speedy switch over. Once Noah completed the call, she led them out of the landing area and past the official-looking buildings nearby, guessing that most of those would be empty with the evacuation. Reaching a junction, the next section appeared wealthier, the space between houses larger, with extensive gardens. Zuri moved on; she knew what she was looking for. When people panicked, they went to two places -

church or hospital. Right now, she wished she had a drone up, another item for their kit list.

But you need to survive before you can thrive. Live and learn.

"Noah, scan the skyline with your rifle sight. See if you can pick out a church or temple roof. Stremall said there should be lots in each city. They all believed different things about the Haven and built big to prove their city was the most spiritual. Maybe look for a hospital building too."

"I'm here, Zuri. Not at full power, but I'm back. Scanning."

"Pleased to hear you Smith, we have people to save." Zuri swapped over the helmet. Smith's targeting would come in handy.

"Eh?" squealed Kinsik. "What—who?"

"It's a computer program, Kinsik. He's called Smith, and he talks through my helmet." Zuri emphasised by tapping Smith's plaque. "He can see and hear much further than us. But his jokes are terrible."

"Heard that! Huge thermal signature five hundred metres southwest, take the next junction left. I have low level thermal everywhere, Zuri. Be careful."

"Let's move," Zuri checked on Kinsik, then broke into a trot. Their sudden move to potency again clearly based on Smith's abilities. With so many solar systems to travel before they were home, they needed to work through the new approaches together to ensure they were effective. That way they could help more people, while increasing their own chances of survival. She had to work on Yasuko to understand the benefits of having the power to make genuine change.

"Hit record, Smith. I want Yasuko to see what we do."

Noah jogged along in the rear, eyes roaming for the Boush threat. He had a gut feeling where they were, feeding in the dark as dawn rose. All around them lay the ripped and melted remains of clothing, shoes and the debris of daily life. Interspersed were the hints of human remains that he trained his eyes to glance over and move on, not letting the horror seep through.

"Kinsik, you okay?" he queried. Kinsik put her thumbs up in response as she ran. At first Noah took that as a positive, but his mind flicked back over his experiences of the last few weeks. Glancing round to check the area, he sped up, ignoring the rasp of his lungs to be beside Kinsik. Tears smudged across her cheeks, wetting the scarf wrapped across her mouth and nose.

"Zuri, stop," he said into the radio. "We need a minute."

Zuri halted, turning round to query Noah, before catching sight of Kinsik. She walked over, open-armed, pulling the teenage girl into her.

Lisilo budi hutendwa. We should do whatever has to be done. But I can't use up people and leave them by the wayside.

"I can't hide the horrors. This is real — but lock it down. If you let this get to you now, you will take others with you." Zuri pulled back, stroking the girl's hair from the side of her face. "We feel what you feel. We are not immune. But we are needed, and we answer the call. If you feel overwhelmed, then you tell us, understand? Tell us so we can act." Kinsik nodded, wiping the tears away. Zuri took another look into the girl's eyes, and satisfied at what she saw there, took up her rifle, assuming the lead again.

After scanning the junction, Zuri stepped out from behind an overturned vehicle. The debris of the voracious creatures' passing lay strewn across the western facing road. And there, about a hundred metres further along, one enormous Boush smothered the entrance to an ornate building, its pseudopods rasping and pulling at the intricate masonry. The thing could find no ingress, yet on it probed, emotionless and persistent in its hunt for food. The windowless building, adorned by a depiction of a Haven upon its cracked tower, defied its hunger.

"No guessing where the people are. And there are multiple smaller Boush along the other walls."

Zuri scanned the street. Buildings ran alongside in tightly packed blocks, their windows and doorways shattered. A clear death-trap should the smaller Boush emerge, but also an opportunity. There was nowhere for the huge Boush to go except straight ahead.

"We clear the doorways and entrances to the north and south, Noah, quietly."

CHAPTER 28

Between Seth City And Ruthyl

Yasuko had never felt tired before, never mind the exhaustion that was setting in now. The constant acceleration, deceleration, stopping, persuading and adapting was more work than she could have imagined. It didn't help that the humans were so stubborn, determined to stay in their homes and defend what was *theirs*. Stremall had changed from a quiet orator to a belligerent one, throwing orders rather than requests, which the people of the villages and towns seemed to respond to more.

It had helped when the Seth soldier Zuri captured had stayed with them. Stremall released the man at the first city drop-off point, but he'd refused to go. He now remained behind when they first encountered a new village, a familiar presence, organising those capable of ground evacuation and seeking any ex-army he could find. Yasuko could now leave small teams at villages and towns to spread the word and get the people moving of their own accord.

Yasuko scanned the radio waves again, still no evacuation message from the cities to the outlying towns and villages. It would save so much time if they could inform the ones closest now, getting them moving so they could focus on the rest. Yasuko made the second big decision of her newfound free will. Hopefully, it would be appreciated more than the first. She tracked the radio wave transmissions, tracing back towards the source from New Halton. Having found the major broadcaster, she sent a simple algorithm worm to seek any secure channels.

The encryptions were tight, but Yasuko was in no mood for subtlety and blew them away before rebuilding the connections herself.

Am I overstepping? There are thousands of lives on the line.

"This is Yasuko of the Earth Explorer spaceship. Am I speaking to the Prime or the King?" the female voice boomed over the throne room PA. Prime Heclite jumped from her chair, her heart racing as the sound reverberated through her skull. The King and Wendyll held their hands over their ears, grimacing against the pain. The other person in the room, the Strategos, or General, of New Halton's remaining armies, strode over to the control panel on the viewscreen, turning it down.

"Too loud, Yasuko. Too loud."

Yasuko adjusted; she'd never invaded another communication system before.

"My apologies." Yasuko's hologram appeared on the viewscreen. "I have an emergency and no time."

"Go ahead," said the King. "We are listening."

"My crew are in Seth. They are requesting you send relief as soon as possible, soldiers and medical help. The city has been overrun, but there are survivors there."

"Yes, of course. My hexacopter reported your earlier message, I have soldiers already on the way," said the King.

"Thank you. I am supporting the evacuation to the south. But there's no response to our actions from the other cities. I could break into their systems, but I doubt they would listen after such an intrusion. The Boush are heading their way, bypassing the fields and seeking the towns and villages for the people within. I can only assume they'll move on to the cities next as a major food source. We need them to evacuate those closest and send out whatever they can for others — and prepare."

"I can call the cities, send them a recording of what has happened here, though I am sure they already know. My guess is that they are doing what we did at first, reacting with a mix of panic, prayer and fear. The biggest question being how to fit all those people in behind their city walls?"

"We get the people there first, it gives them nearly a week to prepare at the speed the Boush are moving, Your Majesty. I can deliver food and supplies to keep the people going."

"Agreed. I will send out the call. What will you do if they don't agree?"

"React. Probably not in a good way." Yasuko's image faded. The last look on her face sent a few shivers down the King's spine.

"That is a woman I would not like to cross," said the King. "Prime, can you get some images of the attacks dialled up, preferably over a few days. Include some of the last gasp actions by Hoplite Stremall. And contact the cities' religious leaders, get them on board. If they understand the cause, they might bring the politicians along with them."

"They are already on board, Your Majesty. They might have been slow to react at first, but they understand the urgency now, and the people's need. It is the politicians dragging their feet."

"I'll draft a message." The King pressed his fingers deep into the corner of his eyes. "Wen, I leave you with Strategos Achaeus to discuss any further help before you go back. I wish you well, my friend."

CHAPTER 29

Seth City

Noah burst through the door, his thermal imaging highlighting the Boush feeding in the middle of the floor, a clasped hand flapping as they sucked at the flesh. The rifle burst took the first out, blasting it backwards into the corridor beyond. The follow up fire split the others in half, the bolts melting the creatures' outer membrane. Noah urgently stepped through the corridor doorway, sweeping the ceiling corners before slamming it shut. This wasn't the time for door-to-door work.

"Clear Zuri."

Zuri prepped Kinsik, the flashbang ready in the girl's hand. Not the procedure she'd have normally chosen, but the girl needed some success after what they'd witnessed.

"Grenade," Kinsik shouted, hurling the grenade through the split door. Zuri waited for the eruption before kicking the door through as the thermal image returned to normal.

"Got four in there, Zuri. Two to the left, one each in the right-hand corners."

She swept the room, picking up on their pulsating signatures and laying fire down on the ones to the left. Their images separated as the bolts seared the gelatinous bodies, their jellied innards washing across the floor. Kinsik was soon at the door, covering her back with the powerful rifle she carried, following through on what Zuri asked her to do. Zuri brought her rifle round, the stunned Boush in the corners suffering the same fate as the others. Kinsik moved in to examine the ruptured internal doorway, with its doorframe melted along with part of the wall. She upended a splintered table, ramming it over the space, and wedged one of its legs as best she could. Temporary, but they wouldn't be here long.

"Clear, Noah."

"Prepping. Zuri I —"

"It has to be Kinsik if this is to work, Noah. You and I know what to do, and at the right time," Zuri's adamant tone rung through her words.

"It's me, Noah. My job." Kinsik spoke with determination too, though Noah took that as false bravado. It wasn't helping.

Noah took out two of his four incendiary grenades made by Yasuko. Illegal in Earth wars, but this was survival and fire was the only tool they were sure killed these things. He also removed the last of his chemical explosive rings, the detonator placed in his pouch pocket. Noah had argued for the ring to be thrown, worrying that the Boush's slime may render it useless, but Zuri felt it was too much risk. He checked outside and found a suitable place clear of vehicles and debris, though it oozed with the Boush's trail. Still the best option. They needed the explosive to erupt upwards, unopposed. Noah placed the ring while gingerly stepping through the slime and signalled to Zuri.

Zuri took out her sidearm, the small energy bolt pistol, and handed it over to Kinsik in exchange for her rifle.

"All you need to do is point and shoot. If this goes wrong, you keep on running until you get to the helipad and call for Yasuko." Zuri gripped her shoulders, looking straight into her eyes. "No risks, understand? Follow the plan." Kinsik nodded, checking the pistol and stepping out of the door, walking towards the quivering mass of death battering the Haven Temple in ravenous hunger.

Zuri and Noah took up position, the emerging sunlight

enough to see by despite the cosmic dust reducing the twin suns' rays. As Kinsik walked, they watched for the smaller Boush that were little threat in tiny numbers, especially at the speed they travelled. Their worries centred on the tendency for them to swarm, and Kinsik getting surrounded or overwhelmed.

The girl kept to a steady pace; enough Zuri hoped to tempt them out. As the first oozed from an upturned vehicle, Noah's burst slammed into it, ending the threat. More slid from shadowed hiding places, and the rain of heated energy poured behind Kinsik, lighting her up as she approached the enormous creature. Each strike caused her to flinch slightly, but she locked them out, keeping her mind focussed ahead.

Ten metres from the throbbing mass, Kinsik stopped, waiting. It would notice her scent eventually, whatever happened, but none of them were prepared to risk the wait. Noah had reassured her it wasn't fast enough to catch her in a straight run, but should she stumble, the ripples it used to surge forward may catch her out. Steady, watch your feet. Kinsik took a half turn, ready to run with one eye on the beast. She put her hand in the air, the signal for five seconds.

On five, Zuri and Noah triggered multiple energy bursts to scorch the enormous mass, the bolts biting deep as the outer membrane parted under the assault. Kinsik felt its attention turn, a tendril reaching out, followed by an enormous feeling of its *regard* falling upon her. She froze, like so many others before her, the weight of being food heavy upon her, like an expectation. Kinsik's mind screamed for her to run; yet her body waited to be consumed. Another burst from behind broke the creature's spell, its tendril twisting as it cooked and smoked under Noah's bolts. And she ran.

The surge from behind pushed and flowed over the debris that Kinsik leapt and hurdled before it. She could hear the ripping as the pseudopods pulled it along, oozing a slime trail the Boush's body rode. A pulsing, gelatinous wave of death. Two more energy bursts sped past her, head high and powerful, hitting home. Yet she could *feel* the creature's hunger and it did not lessen.

Ten metres from Zuri and Noah, a small Boush seeped out from a crack in the road ahead. Kinsik panicked, knowing they were both focussed on the creature behind. She fumbled for her gun, the wild shots melting the road either side of the smaller Boush as she ran. Kinsik dodged to the right, hitting the old slime trail earlier than agreed, but needs must. Too fast, her shoes lost grip, stretching her stride and sending her tumbling to the floor amid the wretched sludge.

Kinsik stole a glance behind as she picked herself up. The Boush, just a few metres back, glowed with ripples of yellow and green. The weight of its craving pressed in on her as it yearned for her protein. She darted to the right again and onto the pavement to get ahead. Not in the plan, but neither was being eaten alive. Ahead of her, the chemical charge sat waiting. That's where she needed to be, and Kinsik sped towards the centre of the road. The baited trap, with her as the tasty morsel. She dodged again, bringing herself back onto the slime trail and leapt the charge as a tendril whipped past her head.

"Kinsik, it's not going on the charge, it's bypassing it. Keep running," bellowed Zuri. But a pseudopod lashed into the girl's helmet, and she fell spinning to the ground.

Noah and Zuri launched the first of their incendiaries, the plan to take out the tail end as the charge disrupted the front. But no choice. They needed to act now as the thing reached out for Kinsik, its *need* pervading the street.

"Grenade," they shouted, and the phosphorus explosive erupted amongst the pulsating waves of its body. The intense heat burnt straight through to the road, and the Boush's body movements dragged more of itself across the chemical fire.

"Grenade," they shouted again, sending the second deep into the main body as the tail burned.

Kinsik felt the tendril's touch. It grabbed around her body, pulling, tasting, then released. She pulled herself through the sludge in fear, slipping and sliding before turning to find several tendrils hanging above her, urging themselves forward, then pulling back like Medusa's hair, snapping and snarling at its prey. And there it stopped, coming no closer, though she was within easy reach. Kinsik raised her slime covered weapon, taking shots at each tentacle, driving them back as she stepped forward. The stench from its burning rear seeped through her scarf, the smoke filling the street. Kinsik could see the mass sliding apart, the individual mini-Boush releasing their mutual hold as they sought to escape. She bent down, pulling the circular charge from the road and throwing it towards the uninjured part of its body.

"Noah, do it," she shouted, hitting the ground in a roll as the explosive erupted, searing into the Boush, spreading chemical fire, heat and pain. And Kinsik ran again.

The chemical explosion ripped into the front of the enormous Boush, rupturing its component parts and splattering the walls of the street. Noah and Zuri immediately moved, striding out of the door, and used their *weapons'* searing air to cook the individual Boush that survived the explosion. They sped from mound to mound, making sure dead was dead before pulling back towards Kinsik at the end of the road. Zuri checked on the teenage girl, while Noah took pot-shots at any Boush they had missed trying to ooze into dark crevices and doorways.

"You've streaked your dust," said Zuri, examining the girl for any injury. The slime, mixed with her dusty stone covering, formed an unpleasant combination. Kinsik looked at her sheepishly, sliding her hands across her neck and pulling back some gloop to examine. "It smells too. Nice."

"It didn't like it, the Boush. It tasted me, my skin, and this." Kinsik showed Zuri the sludge. "And pulled back. I don't think it knew what to make of me. And when I ran through the slime, did you see? It didn't follow."

"Something we may use in the future, Kinsik. Don't let me forget. Tell Yasuko when you see her," said Zuri in reply.

Ahadi ni deni. A promise is a debt, girl. I will not put you through that again.

CHAPTER 30

Seth Foothills

As the hexacopter pulled away, Wendyll led the Phalanx towards the show cave. He activated the radio transmitter, its signal picked up by the booster deep inside the cave mouth. Reya would know in a few minutes, and then it would be a new dawn for their shared people.

No longer the Ghosts Within after today.

The soldiers rolled their heavy barrels of fuel towards the entrance, Wendyll directing them to a specific spot before the long stairway down started. They hefted their flamethrowers next, weapons his home would never have imagined needing before, but vital if they were to survive the coming days.

Wendyll felt the responsive pulse from his transmitter, and the cave section slid inwards. An entrance used for the second time in recent days. Yet before that, shut for four years after Reya first took him down to meet her people. Grey clad Ghosts stepped out, leading motorised trolleys behind them. Wendyll had half-expected a standoff, perhaps a moment of contemplation. Instead, the Ghosts reached out, clasping the forearms of the soldiers with a look of gratitude and faith. The soldiers' responses showing far more emotion than Wendyll would have thought, returning the warmth in equal measure.

In pain, we find mutual need. Hope.

They worked together to heave the barrels and strap them in place. Once the flamethrowers were propped on the last trolley, the group began their descent, with Wendyll leaving a watcher behind for when the rest of the soldiers arrived by road. A small force, but in the confines of the cave system, hopefully enough.

It took an hour to travel the usually hidden ways down to the Gallery, though Wendyll was pleased to see the Ghosts taking a route that avoided their main blockade points. Reya obviously ordering all doorways open until the soldiers passed fully by. In this way, he doubted any of the soldiers could memorise the complete route, and those parts they did recall could be closed and disguised as dead ends. Reya still had some way to go before achieving complete trust of their new allies and, considering the city's attitudes of the past, a sensible choice.

Once at the Gallery, Wendyll enjoyed the moment the soldiers lost themselves in its wonder. He let them drink it in. The shimmering waterfalls and cascading greenery were a powerful message to motivate them in its defence. Something worth saving in the barren land the Boush left behind, as were the children Reya sent to greet them with hugs and smiles.

Never miss an opportunity when survival is at stake.

Wendyll had to admit the genuine awe on the Phalanx's faces was enough evidence for him. They were here for them, and in return, they needed the hand of friendship.

Reya assigned two Ghosts per soldier, forming three teams of six to cover the main caverns that were of concern. The Ghosts would serve alongside the soldiers and learn from their approach. Hopefully ensuring the ability to defend themselves in the future, and possibly to keep a watchful eye on them as well. After they departed for the lower caverns, Wendyll sat with Reya as the school children played.

"You have done well, Wen. The King was pleased to see you?"

"Yes, like time had never passed. There are more soldiers on the way. Possibly we can breathe a little easier when they arrive by road. Have we had any attacks?"

"Many, all connected to the main river tunnel or its subsidiaries. We have lost ten Ghosts, Wen, taken in their sleep. The Boush slide through the smallest cracks, and they seem to thrive in the darkness. But why now? Why has it taken so long?"

"The King believes they are in a hurry, that something is about to happen to the Boush. While I was there, the strangers' ship made contact. The pilot told us they were bypassing the fields and forests in the south, ignoring that bounty, and speeding towards the towns and cities. They seek protein over all else, as if they need the choicest food and quickly."

"Yes. They ignored the plants and went for us instead, which matches what he described. So that makes us a sitting target while we stay here. And if they get in, we are lost."

"They won't leave, you know this."

Reya stood, pacing. "But the children, Wen. We could evacuate them and set traps inside for the Boush with the extra space. Lead them in and exterminate them. It needs to be done before we lose the first child. Once that happens, they'll shut their doors and refuse to come out. Sat in their homes, waiting for their fate."

The scream echoed through the middle gallery, a cry of anguish and pain that stung at Reya's heart. Sprinting for the playground, she picked up a large broom on the way, Wendyll a few paces behind. The children had pulled back from the wall, two small Boush streaming down from the air vent above. One was already on the floor, wrapped around a much-loved animal toy, reacting to its human scent. Reya pinned it in the angle between the floor and wall.

"Wendyll." No need for more words, Wendyll urged the children away as their teachers streamed in, leading them towards a lower stairwell. Taking another broom, he pinned a second Boush as it reached the floor. A few seconds later, a wooden spear pierced the last, the core of burning moss at its tip sending the mold up in flames. Wendyll relaxed as Reya's burned next, followed by his.

Reya looked at Wendyll again, determination and drive powering her mood. "The children, Wen, no choice."

CHAPTER 31

Between Seth City And Ruthyl

Finn shrugged off the covers, pulling out the drip feed while fending off Yasuko's nanobot arms.

"Call them off Yasuko!" he bellowed, losing the battle with one very determined hand that now pinned his arm, jabbing the drip back in.

"Give me one good reason? You're dehydrated and your body has taken a serious amount of abuse. Your leg has only just started healing from the graft, and you have had no consistent sleep for 48 to 72 hours. You have been under high stress and are hallucinating because of a combination of PTSD, battle stress and all the above."

"Granted, but I can't sit here useless. If it was so bad, why haven't you sedated me?"

"Because I don't know what your mental health is like, and right now I'm trying to analyse your brainwaves and electrochemical impulses to see if I can do anything. The Haven scientists had little empathy for their own mental health, never mind for tools of their biosphere development." Yasuko crossed her arms, the look vaguely reminiscent of Zuri's, right down to the eye glare.

"I—I need to be doing something. If you want stress, leave me to do nothing while you all carry on with the mission. I'll be arm wrestling the nanobots in five minutes. Then you'll see how bad I can be. I need to be doing, not thinking. Nothing happened."

"Finn, you are not up to a fight. Rest, get better. There's going to be a series of battles in the next week. They will need you. But after the B—" Finn raised his hands, cutting Yasuko off.

"Smith told you, nothing happened. All is good."

"No, Smith told us you were hallucinating, adding in events that didn't happen. It's classic str—"

Finn gripped the nanobot hand, yanking hard. "No. Stop. It was just dreams. I am fine." Finn's hands wrenched at the nanobot, finally feeling it give.

"You can't deny it, Finn, and if you deny it to Zuri, you'll belittle what you have. I know you're lying and I'm just an AI."

"You...," Finn suddenly gave, tears forming in his eyes. "You are my friend Yasuko, and our shipmate. I'm raging inside, angry at myself, the world, everything." Finn collapsed onto the table, fighting back the overwhelming emotional tide. The dark pressed in.

Yasuko wanted to move closer, feeling the need to give sympathy but not knowing physically how. All she knew were words, and purpose.

Maybe a little purpose will help.

"I can give you a mild sedative, bring the stress hormones down and reduce the symptoms, Finn. But only if you agree to talk to Zuri about this. I can guarantee she will already know. And if you are determined to help, then I have an idea what you could do. But any sign of stress or additional strain on your leg or body you back off. Understand?"

CHAPTER 32

Seth City

Kinsik stared at the Temple steps, trying hard not to, but drawn into thinking about the random objects that littered each one. Metal tablets, pens, watches, torches, a few knives and other weapons amongst them. Each shiny, as if bathed in acid, with every blemish scoured from their surface. Noah moved up by her side, reaching across to squeeze her shoulder, giving her a look that said '*I know and feel it too*' before returning to reduce the small Boush moving along the walls to saggy sacks of water and innards. Zuri was searching the giant double door, stone hewn and rugged. Whatever else these Seth were, they could build a bloody solid door.

"The thermal signature is tremendously strong. There must be thousands in there, Zuri."

"Do they have communication devices, Smith? Any hackable ones?"

"Yes! Absolutely there are and I can hear them. However, I'm not able to break into the phone network. Hang on... there's a radio."

Smith's voice changed, adapting to the authoritative voice he used on the parade ground. He simultaneously translated for Zuri as he spoke.

"Attention! Attention in the Seth Temple. This is the army of New Halton (cough). We are outside your doors; we have neutralised the Boush attacking it. Attention! Attention —" Smith repeated the message three times. *"Zuri, I'm receiving, there's army in there.*

They've acknowledged and are asking us to back off while they look from the roof. All their external electronics have melted."

"Back up Noah, Kinsik. Muzzles down. But eyes open."

They moved swiftly, watching and wary after the past events, with every crevice and shadow a potential problem. Zuri grabbed her binoculars, bringing them up to track the roof and marking the three Boush oozing through the gutters.

"Smith, tell them I'm clearing the decks." With that, Zuri took the creatures out, no other thought than to complete their mission and save lives. As the last burst seared the green body, a helmeted face appeared over the edge.

"You are not New Halton. Identify," shouted the soldier.

"I am Lance Corporal Zuberi of… of… the UK Space Command Reserves sent here by New Halton. We have dispatched the Boush and we need to know whether there are more large strongholds before calling in the evac team."

"The hospital, there are more there. We have wounded inside, but most will be okay for a few hours. There are three Phalanxes left inside - I lost fifty percent of my rear guard seeing the people to safety. I am Hoplite Steen."

"Then we need a plan, Hoplite. One to ensure safety, food and water for your people in there and perhaps some of your soldiers to come with us to the hospital. We have a job to do. You wouldn't have any useful explosives in there, would you?"

"Oh yes, yes, we most certainly do, Zuberi of the UK Space Command."

The huge, vaulted interior of the Temple of Aven reverberated with a massed throng of human life. The mix was all-encompassing, from ragged street urchins through to those clad in the riches of success or inheritance. All were pitching in;

Zuri relieved to see that these people didn't reflect the political expedience she'd witnessed outside the walls. Milling about the residents of Seth were the Hoplite's soldiers, reassuring families about the strangers and the destruction of the Boush outside.

Zuri, Noah and Kinsik sat with the Hoplite Steen and his second in command, Sfendonatai Cremal, a fierce woman covered in the sweat and dirt of war. She was washing her eyes clean of ash and dust as they spoke.

"We holed up as soon as they breached the walls, the Boush—they just kept on coming. Many split at the breach to avoid the flamethrowers, then reformed inside the walls. They move so much faster when they are bigger, they surge like a wave. That change caught many of the people out, thinking they had time and then..." said the Hoplite.

"These people need food and water. There just wasn't the time when we came. The Politico focussed on sending people south or saving their own skins. When we realised they were past our walls, we crammed as many in as we could with the help of the temple priests," continued Cremal.

"You need to go north, towards New Halton. From what we've seen and heard, the Boush are heading south in this larger form, aggressive and on the hunt. If you have radios, I'd suggest contacting New Halton. We already requested help for you, so they may well be on their way with supplies, or even transport," said Zuri.

"They are? We have not cooperated with their army in a long, long time. I can do that, and Sfendonatai Cremal can take charge of clearance, getting us a route out. That leaves you with the hospital? I can provide a Phalanx to get you there, one flamethrower in the group, and we have these." The Hoplite reached behind him, pulling out a bottle stuffed with a rag. "The priests bled their generator, and a broken fuel tank. Any use? That and some explosive grenades," said the Hoplite, gaining a beleaguered smile from Kinsik and Noah.

"Yeah, I reckon they'll do the job," said Noah. "How's your aim, Kinsik?"

"If it means I'm not the bait this time, then my aim is excellent."

CHAPTER 33

New Halton

"Your Majesty," said Prime Heclite. "I have received a message from the Prime at Ruthyl, the southern city by Lake Pern. They wish to discuss the arrival of your security adviser."

"Eh? Is this something you've arranged Heclite, without telling me? Our people are stretched as it is helping the Ghosts and Seth. When did we have time to send an adviser?"

"I didn't, Your Majesty. Maybe we should take the call together? Might be a chance to reinforce your message about the evacuees from Seth who are on the way there. They are on the southern route to the coastal cities. I'd say in two days, they'll be inundated with exhausted and distressed refugees."

"Okay but warn them I'm on the call. The Ruthyl Prime gets panicky when stressed, if I remember correctly."

"You threatened to drop a bomb on him personally if they refused to take evacuees from Jonkren, Your Majesty. About a year ago, I believe."

"Did I? My memory seems a little vague about that time. We were *very* busy."

What a mad time that was, the thousands streaming across the Jonkren Passage with nowhere else to go to.

The Prime spoke briefly into his mobile device, before pointing to the screen. "It's coming up now. I have warned the man, but I can't guarantee he won't be jumpy." The screen against the wall briefly flickered and a bald man dressed in a heavy red formal robe appeared. His tense face and posture further punctuated by the clasped hands in front of him. "Ah, Prime Brenan, so good to see you," said Heclite. "I do hope that you are keeping well."

"I try, Prime Heclite, though there are few days of rest this wet season. Your Majesty, it's a pleasure to meet with you again."

"And you, Prime Brenan, did I ever say thank you for accepting the survivors from Jonkren? If not, then please accept my deepest thanks," King Paledine smiled graciously as he spoke.

Most have been working in your mobile farms for a pittance.

"They have settled well, though it appears they may well have jumped back into the firing line. I have a man here claiming to be your adviser on *'defence against the Boush'*. Must say he turned up in that ship we heard rumours about. Is it yours?" The Prime showed a video in the top corner of his screen, Yasuko's ship landing in front of their walls, and the man Finn limping as he exited in their full armour.

Prime Heclite slipped a piece of paper over to Paledine, the words *Lance Corporal Finn* written upon it.

"The ship? No, but they helped fight off the Boush attack. A hero, you would say, alongside his squad. They come from another planet, as mad as that seems, but they've met the Aven." Heclite placed her hands on her heart when the King mentioned the Aven, Brenan following suit. "And are as bloody-minded about helping people as I am. Wait till you meet the ship's Pedon, their pilot, not one I'd cross."

"So, you would say we should listen? We are—err—proficient in the ways of war, Your Majesty."

"Prime Brenan, war is not an adequate term for what you are about to face. We sent you the film of the attack on us. The Boush decimated Jonkren and its cities, Lance Corporal Finn and his people wish to help. I'd listen. Seth's now overrun, and they boasted about their professional army to anyone and everyone. Always take heed of other people's perspective and only dismiss it once it's understood. And remember, you have hundreds, if not thousands of refugees coming your way, and there's no one else but you to protect them." King Paledine eased back in his chair, hoping the Ruthyl Prime had the sense to at least ask for some help.

"Thank you, Your Majesty. I will take your words into consideration. May the Aven protect you," said Brenan as he signed off.

"Well, if they don't get their act together, we could be looking at another massacre, Heclite. They will take them in, won't they? The refugees?"

"You would hope so, Your Majesty. I have had a word in the right ear, as requested. But we all react differently when under pressure."

CHAPTER 34

Ruthyl

Finn examined the mechanism on the flamethrower attached to the city walls. Similar in style to that of Seth, the crane smoothly eased out over the battlement and could be fired down the line of the wall at an excellent angle to get under the Boush's pseudopods, as they pulled themselves up. The angle had more scope for adjustment than Stremall's at New Halton. However, he could immediately see the fuel lines were thinner, the muzzle designed for distance over volume. Though that would have its uses, once the enormous things were on the wall, the volume of fire was key. Just look at the effect Yasuko's engines had with their intensity. He scanned the rest of the battlement, hoping to see perhaps a wider variety of the weapons so they could vary the tactics, but they all appeared the same.

"Well, Lance Corporal Finn," said Assistant Prime Tethin, "Fine beasts, aren't they? Built in my brother's factory. Technically above anything at New Halton."

Finn looked the older woman up and down. Fine clothes and manicured hands hid a wily politician underneath. She had assessed him in seconds and decided to give him the time of day. At least that was a start.

Ah well, either she'll throw me off the walls or feed me to the Boush. Probably both.

"Technically, I couldn't say. But these designs are for distance as far as I can tell. That might be an issue when they're crawling up your walls. I fought at New Halton alongside Hoplite Stremall, and the volume of fire won the day. Can I see a demonstration?"

"Certainly," replied Tethin, and spoke to the Hoplite in charge. The following demonstration didn't allay his fears. They were good, distance wise, but the flow of fire was low. If the Boush were as adaptive as Yasuko had warned him about on the way, then there needed to be more.

"If I said you have a problem, would you listen? Or am I wasting my time?" asked Finn, wondering how far it was down to the base of the walls and wincing as he readjusted his leg.

"I would choose to listen. Go ahead."

"Okay, the flamethrowers won't have the capacity of fire you need. Volume is essential, especially when they are close. You have to hit them hard, and those throwers can't do that. I think you need to adapt them in your brother's factory ASAP."

Wait for it.

"My brother's factory? I must have misspoken," said the Assistant Prime, a smile on her face, "I meant the factories belonging to Prime Brenan's brother. You, Lance Corporal Finn, now have my ear and there aren't many people who can say that." Finn shook his head in response. This woman had everyone's measure.

"If that's the case, these are your key priority, but you are in serious trouble." Finn lent over the wall, risking more pain as he pointed down. "The Boush I fought were nearly over New Halton's walls when we took them down, and yours are maybe five metres shorter. I flew over Seth's walls, and these seem a similar height. How long did they last?"

"Not one day, Lance Corporal, as well you know. You were on the inside, and no, I don't want to know why you are shaking or look on the verge of collapse." Finn raised his eyebrows, though not in the least bit surprised about this woman's intelligence.

"I just want to know how to stop the Boush, and a man who's fought on the walls of New Halton and subsequently survived Seth's death-trap, is a good start. We have two days before the refugees arrive, and maybe three before the Boush. I require plans, Lance Corporal Finn. I have grandchildren to defend, and we can't keep sending everyone on to the next city. There's no more room."

"Okay, I'll look into the walls, as I may have an idea being Scottish and all. From you I need to know the volume of available flamethrower fuel, and how many helicopters you have still flying, *and* how we are going to get your Prime to turn the manufacturing over for those flamethrowers."

"Now?"

"Now."

"You, Finn, are a man I could get to like."

CHAPTER 35

Seth City

Zuri stood watch next to Kinsik and Noah as the Phalanx took point, attempting to draw the smaller Boush out, working their way past the infestation towards the hospital. They all struggled with the sights and smells on route. The smaller, slow-moving Boush feasted upon bodies strewn across the roads, attempting to stay out of the light, yet their hunger forcing them to reach longingly from cracks and beneath cars, even from under the bodies themselves. The constant noise of grazing pseudopods tearing and melting through flesh and bone, drove the newly formed team to burn their way through, using up precious fuel, but desperate to eradicate the creatures and their grisly work. Of course, removing the smaller slime molds meant they didn't leave a potential enemy behind on their return route.

Along the way, they came across the occasional group of desperate citizens, awash with relief, waving from sealed houses or running across the streets to meet them. Those safe inside they ordered to stay, the rest were sent back along the cleared roads towards the sanctuary of the stone temple. After the first group, the Phalanx leader, Sfendonatai Hander, radioed back to the Hoplite, explaining what was happening. The Hoplite's mood lifted further by the news of survivors, though he remained concerned about food and clean water.

However, the trickle of people soon dropped off as they closed in on the hospital. The people there must have crowded the roads, frantic, and the resultant crush had become a killing ground. A sea of yellow and green heaved as hundreds of Boush oozed amongst the vehicles, eager to eat.

Kinsik turned to Noah and hid her eyes against his shoulder, unable to cope with the sheer death that seethed around her. Zuri surveyed the scene, her mouth open with the horror, revolted. Wrenching her eyes away, she moved beside Noah, her look questioning his emotional state, and receiving a nod in reply.

"I—I can't—I don't…" Sfendonatai Hander trailed off, unable to articulate what was happening, or what to do next.

"We bring the fire. That's what we do, but we need a clear way through. Anyone drive a truck?" Zuri said, pointing to the large tanker parked at the edge of the traffic jam. "With enough momentum, it might get us through most of the way, especially if we can find a relatively weak point. Then we hit the Boush along the route with our weapons, save the fuel bombs and flamethrower for what's inside."

"I may be able to," said the Phalanx soldier carrying the flamethrower. "I was a firefighter before being drafted. Let's hope the keys are inside. Lendrick's the name." Zuri looked the woman up and down. Memories of Luther back on earth came flooding back. A trainee lost to !Nais's soldier gone bad, a firefighter playing soldier in a Scottish forest. And now here she was, a few months later, on a different planet hundreds of light years from home, yet still fighting for what was right.

Kuwa geuzo unalotaka kuona duniani. Be the change you want to see in the world.

Miss you, momma.

Noah and Zuri worked their way around the tanker, the Phalanx soldiers buddying up as they used the extreme heat from their *weapons* to clear the engine of the few hiding smaller Boush. The surrounding feast far too tempting to keep them in the shadows for long.

"There's a spot about fifty metres that way where the cars are nose to tail and more angled. I reckon the tanker could push a good way in, then maybe back up and ram the rest. What's in the tank?" said Sfendonatai Hander returning from a swift scouting mission. His brief panic over now he had a purpose, and a little hope. Using it to wall away the overwhelming sight and smell of the feasting creatures.

"I don't know your written language, but I was told it's milk, and milk is heavy. That should help," said Noah, returning from his efforts clearing the Boush.

The ex-firefighter took a seat at the wheel, the Sfendonatai having checked the cab first before taking the shotgun seat. The keys were in the ignition, an abandoned vehicle whose driver was either a likely meal or safe inside the hospital. Time to find out. The engine fired up first time, thrumming with promised power. Finding first gear, the tanker moved forward, easing its way along the road before turning into the section indicated by Hander. The tanker nudged into the cars as it straightened, the driver carefully judging the weight of liquid sloshing around in the tank, unbalancing the rear. She gunned the engine once straight, and the liquid settled, maximising the torque as the truck pushed its way through the weak spot in the jam. The huge tyres gripped the road, squelching through the mix of Boush and bodies as the power of the engine heaved against the metal chassis of the vehicles. About twenty metres in, the sheer weight of the cars forced against each other stopped their progress. Lendrick checked behind as they reversed back, and using the extra momentum, rammed the blockage to make a few more metres. They repeated this method, gaining another ten before coming to a halt twenty metres short of the hospital garden wall that marked the end of the road.

"I reckon we could make a full charge in and get through, Sfendonatai, but you have to get out first. This thing's a swine to drive with its high centre of gravity. It may well tip over. You need to be on the outside to get me out. And you don't leave me to those things, even if I'm trapped. Got me?" Hander nodded, a grim smile as he gripped the woman's arm. No words necessary.

After reversing back the full distance out of the jam, the Sfendonatai jumped from the cab under cover of his men, before waving them into position. Noah and Zuri took point, their *weapons* ready to clear any Boush that wandered onto the newly made path. The tanker engine roared, and accelerated forward, the weight dragging it back but essential as Lendrick aimed to smash a way through. Shifting gears, the truck crashed into the last few cars, metal grinding as the cab lifted on impact. The wheels, returning to the road, gripped and drove the machine on. The tanker started to jack-knife, but the weight drove the machine onwards, piercing the last few metres and smashing into the low brick wall beyond. As the momentum of the liquid finally told, the trailer flipped over onto the cars behind, twisting the coupling and dragging the cab over to rest against the newly demolished wall.

Noah and Zuri pounded down the path, briefly stopping to kill Boush along the way, with the Phalanx in pursuit behind. By the time they arrived at the truck, milk was spurting from the tank, with a grateful but battered and bruised driver emerging, nursing a broken arm. They were through.

CHAPTER 36

Cave Complex, Seth Foothills

Wendyll ran his fingers through his remaining wisps of hair. The radio conversation with the New Halton soldiers arriving via the road route hadn't improved his mood. They were a day distant after vehicle issues with the dust, and with the gathering children in the show cave, he needed to get moving as soon as possible. At least King Paledine agreed to send additional vehicles to pick them up, it was just going to take a little time. The Boush attacks had shown them they could avoid the smaller ones if they kept moving. Waiting, however, would be a death sentence for some.

Down below, the Boush had increased in number, using the air duct system to move about the whole of the City Within. They emerged through the grates in numbers, almost coordinated, rather than seeking prey alone. How could they not be a thinking animal? He'd heard stories of Jonkren, how the Boush had first arrived with the cosmic dust, the spores germinating into a slime mold that rapidly spread and engulfed the forests and fields. For years they battled to grow food, often at the brink of starvation. They survived by using chemical sprays, frequently changing the combinations as the mold adapted. Then, during a respite from the dust cloud and under the full light of their suns, the mold had fruited, forming red puffballs that fired fine white spores to float over Jonkren on the winds.

Within weeks the Boush appeared. They ate away at all life,

with animals and humans suddenly on the menu. Even then, the people had time to reach places of safety as the slow-moving molds took on easy prey. Rumours spread they could problem solve, find ways into barns and homes that no one had thought possible. Before long, panic truly set in, and refugees from Jonkren flowed through the port at New Halton, desperate unhomed people looking for respite. But those that stayed behind reported the Boush's most voracious form in the last year, merging to form huge colonies as their appetites grew, and then Jonkren fell silent. Now those Jonkren refugees lay between Seth and the southern cities, in shanty towns that would be easy pickings.

If they really do exist, then may the Aven help us. We have such little time left.

"Okay, form up children. In pairs, everyone must have a partner. Yes, Emile, boys can partner with girls, they don't bite. You have seen the Boush below, so you know why we are walking in the light above. We should be safe, but keep your eyes out on stalks, help each other. Understand? And we go to the toilet together, when adults have checked areas, not when you feel like nipping off. No one is to be alone." Wendyll passed the signal down the line, the teachers and volunteer adults all carrying stacks of hardened root canes with dried Yernt moss wrapped around. On their backs were packs full of extra moss if needed.

Wendyll gave a last signal to the parents carrying their youngest in baby slings, or on wheeled trolleys, before setting off. Scattered amongst the convoy were remnants of the Ghost Guard, volunteer men and women who carried the powerful rifles they favoured, though they had been of little use defending the City Within. At least their aura of authority would encourage the wilful inhabitants to follow his rules as they walked towards salvation.

CHAPTER 37

Ruthyl

Yasuko brought the ship to a stop outside the walls of Ruthyl, and with the doors opening, the townspeople from Porb filed out, dazed by their circumstances and the speed of their journey. Yasuko checked her fuel levels, the palladium nearly out and her mass close to depletion - flying through an atmosphere taking its toll on already depleted resources. This group numbered over two hundred, and in all she'd transported thousands to the city and set thousands more on the journey with Stremall's help. But she was close to done and soon the internal systems would cannibalise the ship to keep it going.

"Yasuko," called Finn as he stepped on board, "have you another drip pack for me?" The last of her nano-arms emerged from the floor at Finn's feet, the clear liquid bag in its hand. Finn changed over his near empty bag, the valve system quick and easy to use. "Thank you."

"That's the last. You should be rehydrated enough when that's finished, and you've reached your limit with the anxiety drugs." Yasuko's hologram appeared in front of Finn, concern in her posture. "And I'm done, Finn, there's little fuel left, or palladium to manufacture more."

"Ah," said Finn, "I was going to ask you to fetch the mining equipment. If we can dig a moat around the city walls, I think we could give them a much bigger chance. They have enough fuel to keep the flamethrowers going, but the walls are are too low." Finn paused for a second, an idea forming. "What if the city has palladium to spare? How much would you need to get you there and back?"

"About 20kg would do it, but—"

"I know a woman who can do wonders. Wait for me." Finn strode out of the ship door, talking animatedly into his radio. Yasuko could see his self-belief returning. The shadow of a man she'd dropped off a few hours before was a far cry from the one now negotiating on the radio. But then, here she was too with a renewed purpose, making a difference to this world and its people. The influence of these humans, her friends, was difficult to measure. Somehow their determination had crept into her systems, and despite their apparent desire to be prepared for any fight, their need to help impacted all those around them, and her understanding of *self.*

Yasuko responded to a sensor alert, checking over the information coming in from the atmosphere. The dust cloud was thinning, the predicted edge appearing in three days, and likely clear by the seventh. Something nagged at her. She knew it was important, but she didn't have enough information to know why.

Finn returned. "I'll have it in three hours, Yasuko, and then we need that mining equipment. We only have two more days to prepare before the Boush horde hit, and from your reports we're looking at twenty of the giants, with more likely to join them. How long do you estimate before the rest reach the southern cities?"

"I'd say five days if the towns are clear, six if they feed on the way. The call is out. The King was true to his word and the political leaders in the south are reacting, but they do not have city walls, Finn. If I can get fuelled up, maybe I can help, but I fear for them."

"Okay, I have a plan for that. But it'll only provide a delay once we've defended here and if we can get the others to listen. While they load the palladium, can you send the King another message for those cities?"

CHAPTER 38

Seth City

Gasping for breath, Zuri and her team slammed into the wall on either side of the hospital doors. Their run from the crashed tanker interrupted by a group of Boush flowing to form a colony behind them, responding to the presence of food. Their cue to move, and move quickly, their *weapons of choice* far less effective against the faster, larger versions of the ravenous slime. Hander supported the driver on the run as she struggled with a broken forearm, smashed by the steering wheel when the tanker crashed into the last cars.

The entrance door's broken glass was edged with dried slime, and half-consumed bodies lay within. Looking down the main corridor, Zuri felt a sense of foreboding, every table and chair upturned and scorched, reflective of a running battle with the Boush.

"Smith?"

"Sensors are telling me there are two larger Boush on this floor, not the house size ones, about half that. One in this main corridor and the other in the reception area to the right as you go in. I am getting a gap along that main corridor, and air movement around it. I'm guessing that's a stairwell."

Zuri relayed Smith's information to the Phalanx.

"Keep talking to me, Smith. Anything that sets the alarm bells off," said Zuri, then switching to the Phalanx leader. "Hander, are we splitting up? You could take the main corridor with the flamethrower as backup, we'll deal with the one in reception." Hander nodded, taking his team forward while leaving the injured ex-firefighter behind at the entrance for now. The Phalanx moved, two at the front with the heavy rifles, and two behind carrying Molotovs, ready to light and throw. To the rear, a nervous-looking soldier with Lendrick's flamethrower walked behind, eyes constantly roaming.

Zuri handed Kinsik their Molotovs, the girl ready as they moved out to the right and slipped inside the entrance. The corridor opened out after three metres, the space covered in shattered and burnt chairs. The brick reception desk stretched along the back, about four metres long, covered in fresh, wet slime. Behind, they could see the ripple of yellow and green as the Boush focussed on whatever meal lay beyond the counter.

"Smith?" whispered Zuri, signalling stop.

"Just the one, but there's a room behind with a shut door. Can't sense anything in there, probably empty, but most of the windows are shattered on this floor."

"So, they could be in there." Zuri signalled for Kinsik to come forward. Flanked by Noah, the girl placed a bottle on the floor and lit another before throwing it the five metres required. It bounced off the far edge of the counter and shattered its flaming contents over the feeding Boush. Rearing up, the giant slime mold sent out tendrils searching for the source of its destruction. Kinsik immediately threw the second bottle, the fuel alight and spilling over the mold's underside. The creature made to stretch over the counter but, sensing the burning fuel, a ripple spread through it and an exodus of smaller Boush ensued, desperate to get away from heat and flame. Zuri and Noah moved in, the super-heated air instantly drying out the Boush as they fled.

Noah looked through the closed door, catching sight of the tangled mess of corpses within. Smaller Boush mingled amongst them.

"There's nothing we can do for them; the door keeps them away from us. We move on," said Zuri, pulling him away as Kinsik prepped her next bottles.

They moved towards the main corridor, again with Zuri and Noah in the lead, to be greeted by smaller Boush fleeing the burning Hander's squad had laid down. Noah and Zuri reduced the stragglers to husks and joined the Phalanx.

"Sit rep?" said Zuri.

"Eh?" replied Hander.

"What's happened here? What do we know?"

"This Boush was battering at the metal corridor doors. They're chained and padlocked tight, no cracks through. We found that space in the wall, two in fact, a lift that's stopped above this floor and the stairwell—no door left and half-dried slime all over the stairs, up and down," said Hander.

"You want up or down?" asked Zuri, knowing the answer.

"Up, people go up when scared."

"Okay, down it is. What about Lendrick?"

"Leave her here, watching this place. She can radio me if there's an issue." Hander fetched the injured woman over, talking her through the orders. Noah looked questioningly at Zuri, showing his sidearm. Zuri gave a reluctant shake of her head. Kinsik currently had hers and she would not risk lessening their firepower further.

Me and mine first, and a promise to a Ghost.

Lendrick drew out her own sidearm, a typical handgun, that she held in her right hand. Two fuel-laden bottles at her side. With that, Hander moved out cautiously, heading up the stairs as Zuri led her team down. They couldn't risk these things at their backs.

They moved below ground level, the ambient light enough to see by at first, but wishing for a steadier light, Zuri led the way. She switched to thermal as the stairs ended at a caved in doorway, the brick sides covered in wetter slime than the stairs. No thermal signatures yet.

"That's the storage area, loads of boxes and containers, plus another room that is showing a lot of heat. Boiler room maybe?"

Zuri eased to the side of the door while wishing, not for the first time, that Finn had sanctioned drones. There was a battle she would win after returning to the ship, sense over irrational decisions. She popped her mirror sight into position, manoeuvring the rifle round with her thermal HUD still on. Multiple small signals, slightly colder than the floor and walls, showed up, and one much bigger.

"There's a big one for you, Kinsik. We'll hold the others off while you use that arm. It's to the right, about ten metres. We'll cover first while you step out and throw. We've time, so don't rush."

Haraka haraka haina baraka. Hurry, hurry has no blessing. Don't waste the bottles.

Zuri stepped out, taking a low crouch and focussing her rifle on the large Boush feeding on an open medical waste container. Noah moved behind, sweeping the rear for any concerns. After a few seconds, Kinsik lit her first bottle. Standing behind Zuri, she threw, releasing a squeal of frustration as the burning rag flew out from the glass neck before it smashed in front of the unconcerned Boush. Kinsik swore, though the translator didn't respond. Stuffing the rag further in, Kinsik threw the newly lit bottle, rewarded by an eruption of flame and fuel. The Boush lit up; the flames running along its entire body.

"Zuri, trouble to the right."

She swivelled as a six-metre-long Boush emerged from a large freezer and surged across the short distance towards her.

"Get Kinsik out!" she ordered, hitting the advancing Boush with a blast of scorching air. Hearing the scrambling behind her, Zuri fired again, with the creature now two metres away and in her range. The heat dried up a central lump, but the six-metre-long gelatinous creature didn't flinch as its wave like ripples heaved forward again. Zuri spun, trying to make it to the doorway as the pseudopods shot out and attached to the door frame, sucking its mass forward to envelop her back.

Zuri's scream stung Noah's ears as she reached the door, her white-knuckled hands gripping the brickwork as she dropped her *weapon* to ride on its sling. He pushed his rifle past her body, muzzle amongst the mass of tearing tendrils and melting slime. He fired the super-heated air into its centre, then up towards the pseudopods ripping at her back. Zuri drew in another breath, her scream of agony and effort mingling as she ripped herself clear of the Boush, leaving behind a mix of ceramic plate, Kevlar and the green kinetic gel. Noah fired another volley.

"Get up the stairs, go!" he shouted, backing up and laying withering fire on the Boush that oozed through the doorway, stretching out with keening hunger, its newly formed tentacles surging towards him. Two energy bolts fizzed over his shoulder, ending their grasping reach, and Noah backtracked up the steps.

"Run," shouted Kinsik as she threw her last Molotov towards the Boush, the heat and flame causing it to recoil.

CHAPTER 39

Outside Of The Seth Foothills,
Northern Road To New Halton

Wendyll brought the children and their supporting adults to a halt. They'd been following the road for a good five kilometres now, and the children needed rest. The trolleys had worked well; the children taking it in turns for short stints with friends to lift their spirits, though the adults pulling them needed just as many breaks. Stretching back, he judged the line of humanity to be two hundred and fifty strong, with the teenagers back at the City Within, adding the same number again. The Ghosts had always preferred to nurture a few children rather than have huge broods, but that made each one even more precious.

The ragtag convoy split into smaller groups. The adults supervising as the children took turns relieving themselves in the fields. As he scanned the horizon, Wendyll realised where they were. Chance had brought them to a halt on his old fields. The last farm he had overseen before Reya persuaded him to join the Ghosts, those nights when the meteor showers meant something other than death. The mobile homestead had been returned years ago to New Halton for another family to rent, but what he would give for one now to carry his charges to sanctuary.

Wendyll caught sight of a strange mound out in the barren field to the west, something new to his eye, though memory can always play tricks. He pulled up his belt, the handgun at his side next to useless in his hands, but a reassurance. Setting off across the mud to investigate, he signalled his intent to the second-in-command. After a good ten minutes of mud and husks, Wendyll reached the edge of the mound. The hardened material crusted into concentric ripples as it rose from the ground. Wendyll scanned the area, and satisfied no Boush were around, he tested the crust with his weight before proceeding upwards towards its top. Each step seemed to press slightly inwards, but whatever was underneath gave just enough that he didn't break through. At the top was a bulbous cap, and through its newly formed sheer crust he could see the too familiar swirl of yellow and green. Wendyll's blood pulsed as realisation struck. The entire mound must have been forty metres across, and about eight high, a little more than the colossal Boush colony Stremall had described assaulting the southern wall of New Halton.

Backing off slowly, Wendyll retraced his steps, each one greeted with a tremor through the hardened skin of the Boush. Taking his final step, Wendyll discovered a new turn of speed as he flew across the mud-caked field, feeling the non-existent breath of a Boush on his neck. Arriving back with his charges, desperate lungs screamed for air, the fear on his face not helping their anxious response to the mud-soaked leader. Wendyll rested his hand on the shoulder of his second-in-command, wheezing but reassured that there was nothing chasing him, just the shock of what he'd encountered.

Reforming their convoy, they set off once again, hopefully just hours from meeting up with the soldiers sent by King Paledine, and the sense of security that might afford, with a tale to tell.

CHAPTER 40

Ruthyl

Finn examined the mining vehicles as they vacated the hold of the ship, ticking off their roles and usefulness in his mind. The mixture of robotic excavators, enormous trucks and powerful digging machines were a welcome sight. Yasuko set them to work immediately, taking the surface soil first, and then digging deeper, targeting where her ground penetrating radar gave hope of depth at the base of the walls. There would be shallower sections where the rock layer rose to the surface, but in between the depth gave Finn's plan a chance of succeeding. Yasuko slaved the machines to Finn's radio and a tablet she provided, instructing them to follow his commands as she uploaded an English language algorithm into all their systems. These changes equated to the last of the promised palladium, and though she gathered a little on her brief visit to the mines, she was desperate for much more on her return.

Yasuko wanted to help with the redesign of the flamethrowers, but she simply didn't have the resources for any more manufacturing, and Finn had insisted it was in hand. Certainly, he appeared to have the support of the people. The palladium arrived on time, delivered by a formidable woman, Assistant Prime Tethin, who commanded those around her with an aura of respect. What fascinated Yasuko were the three quadcopters from a southern city, politicians and Kings arriving to view the city's new defences taking shape. Ideas they may action themselves on their return.

But why look for ideas so late? Why hadn't they prepared? Do I assume too much about humans?

At least they would see Finn's new contraption - a bucket with a valve at the rear. If it worked, then lit fuel would leak from the back, providing an ability to burn the Boush from a safe distance. The valve was under Ruthyl's design team's eyes right now, but Yasuko could see it working, a shame Noah wasn't there to help.

"Finn, I'm going to have to head back to New Halton. I'm nearly spent."

"Okay, Yasuko, you've achieved great things here. Safe journey and keep in touch," he replied as Yasuko rose from the ground, her engines complaining as she kept the fuel as sparse as she dare.

What is it the humans say? Crossing my fingers on this one.

CHAPTER 41

Seth City

Noah watched the Boush burn, rifle ready should anything come through the door, Kinsik searching through his backpack for the last two Molotov cocktails. The remains of Zuri's pack lay aflame amongst the shredded creature, the Molotov bottles exploding as the flames from Kinsik's last throw reached them. Noah had dodged most of the eruption, putting out a few flames that stuck to his armoured legs. Kinsik set the retrieved bottles down, and turned to Zuri who sat, ashen-faced, on the step above.

"Can I look?" Kinsik asked, seeking Zuri's reassurance to check any wounds. Zuri pivoted on the step, wincing as she did so, but unsure of the source of the pain. Kinsik prodded amongst the ruins of the armour to find little remained of the back plates or the gel between them. Here and there the Boush had gotten through – livid, raw sections where it had pulled off skin, and others, scorch marked and blistered after contact with the yellow secondary slime that broke its food down. Kinsik cleaned these with anaesthetic wipes from Zuri's remaining belt pouch. Each press being rewarded with a hiss of pain.

"Thank you," Kinsik said as she removed the last of the drying yellow substance, "for getting me out first. Without this armour you would be mostly dead."

"You mean dead?"

"No. I mean, like those people we passed. Eaten alive, mostly dead before being fully dead." Kinsik paused. "I hope my people are okay. There are few Ghosts like me. Most think even fishing is barbaric."

"There are few people like you anywhere, Kinsik. You have stood alongside us despite the fearful things I asked you to do, and the horrors we have come through. Many would have frozen or run." Zuri winced as her skin stretched. The chemical burns were the worst.

"Will we win? Will we ever get rid of these things?"

Zuri squeezed her hand in reply. What answer could she give that wasn't a lie?

"Maybe, but if we stop trying, then it's definitely a *no*. Come on, we need to check that room. Noah?"

"Yes, Zuri. Ready, and I think I'm the one going in first. Your armour is compromised."

"Agreed, for now. Lead the way."

Noah took point, Zuri slightly behind and walking with care as her skin stretched along the burn marks.

"Clear of the bigger Boush, Zuri. That one went up in flames too. But there are more freezers down there, shielded against my sensors. I'm sor—"

"Stow it, Smith, no one to blame. We are all in this together."

"The smaller Boush are forming up. I'd suggest you go in quick to take them out, before they do."

"Okay, Noah survey the room, we go on your say-so. Kinsik, save the bottles in case we get a big one."

Noah switched to thermal and then night vision, as he realised the burning Boush and fuel negated its usefulness. The mirror sight showed the forming Boush, ten of the smaller molds merging towards each other. Signalling in, he went through with Zuri at his back, the super-hot air striking the group and drying them up as they worked in unison.

"More behind the racks to the left, forming up, but watch that freezer nearby."

Noah led the way, glancing into the freezer, muzzle first, and wishing he hadn't, moving on from the melted bags of cadavers and body parts within. On arriving at the corner of the racks, another Boush colony rose menacingly from the floor. Zuri dropped to the ground, laying down supporting fire with energy bolts from under the rack's lowest shelf as Noah approached. His scorching air withering the Boush to husks as they tried desperately to escape via the faster, larger form. If you could draw these things out, they were so much easier to kill.

"Racks clear. Any more Smith?" asked Noah as the last Boush fell under his weapon.

"Not here. The only place left is that boiler room. I can't sense anything through that heat."

"Zuri?"

"We go in, Noah. Can't leave anything behind us, but it's unlikely there'll be any Boush." Noah nodded, unlikely but not impossible, and he stalked across the room checking each unpleasant freezer a second time as he went. Reaching the warm door, he placed his hand against it, feeling the vibration of the boiler behind. Trying the handle, it wouldn't give, not locked but blocked by something. Hopeful, he rapped on the door.

"Anyone in there? We are soldiers," he shouted, then repeated the rapping. Noah felt the handle give, and it swung open. On the floor lay a young boy, no older than ten years old, his skin glowing red and his eyes sunken with lips cracked. As Noah stepped in to take the boy in his arms, more figures came into focus. Bodies lying heaped together, all children and all alive, but only just.

"Kinsik, any water back there? And salt. We need salt too, and sugar will help," asked Noah as Zuri pushed past, moving amongst the children, taking each by the wrist, murmuring words of reassurance. Amongst the death of the day, Noah could feel relief well from his heart, tears threatening to dissolve the wall he'd put up.

Push that down, Noah. These people need you now, and fully focussed.

Kinsik brought back some large bottles of distilled water. Not the best, but the salt tablets she brought would help. They moved the children out of the room, away from the heat, slowly giving each child drops of water.

"Lance Corporal Zuberi, you okay in there?" Hander's voice echoed down the stairwell.

"We have some children, Hander, we need water," she said.

"On my way." Orders barked out, followed by the thump of boots on the stairwell as the Phalanx descended, the soldiers appearing dishevelled, uniforms ripped, with chemical scorch marks exposed on arms and legs.

Zuri saw their faces crumple, tears not held back as they knelt amongst the children, canteens in hand.

"No one... no one at all up there. Just death, every door broken through. We are out of fuel, but we took down the larger Boush before it could do any more damage." Hander looked harrowed. Whatever he'd seen on the floor above marked him now, probably forever. Before Zuri could reply, he'd knelt amongst the children as they came round from their stupor, concerned, but relieved they were alive.

"Smith." Zuri tapped her helmet. "Anything around here flammable?" Noah perked up at her words, a slight smile on his face despite Hander's news.

"Yeah, medical alcohol. That'll burn well, and if we had some thickening agent like a petroleum jelly, it'd be even better. Even hand sanitiser would do it."

"Hander, Lendrick, can you help us gather some flammable

supplies? We can't read your language."

CHAPTER 42

Outside Of The Seth Foothills, Northern Road To New Halton

Wendyll raised the hardened root, the moss alight, prodding at the mold as it slid from the ditch at the side of the road. The children had all pulled into the middle, adults on the outside prodding and poking, as the small Boush emerged hungry but slow in their pursuit of agile prey. Both sides were now unsafe, thirty or forty of the creatures slithering towards them as Wendyll urged his people onward, to follow behind his second-in-command. The Boush were risking the light despite their diminutive size, their impulse to feed rising in urgency. They were herding the convoy, and if they merged, there would be trouble.

"Cover the sides, get the children through, then form up behind them. Fend the damn things off," he shouted down the radio, transmitting wide in the hope The New Halton soldiers may be close. "None get through, Talik, Mander and Threll. You're on the back line. See a gap, plug it. One gets through, kill it. None shall pass."

Wendyll speared one of the gelatinous things, setting it alight and pleased to see it wither under the flame. Another two flared up nearby, telling a tale of the molds getting ever closer as Wendyll insisted the children walked, not ran. If panic set in, they'd lose them to the fields, following each other like sheep to who knows what fate.

The Boush squeezed together, their thin, outer membrane

wall, merging with their neighbours. Growing mold by mold into a pulsating menacing mass as more emerged from the fields.

"Together, we strike the large one on my call. Three, two, one now." Four of the teachers struck out, spearing the ever-growing blob simultaneously, the moss igniting sections, but not enough for it to catch fully alight. A strong pulse surged through it and a pseudopod whipped out, catching Talik on his hip as he joined the fray. The scream pierced the night, the rasping of flesh punctuated by the searing of the bone beneath. Talik fell, knocking two others over, and the mold threw more tendrils out, sucking at their bodies, hunting the protein within. More agonised shouts echoed across the road and the ripple of anxiety reached the children's feet as they panicked.

Wendyll stabbed the tendril attached to Talik, dragging him back as yet another lashed out from the creature to rip at his chest, pulling him in towards the pulsating, slime covered underside of the ravenous mold. Wendyll felt the tear as Talik's shirt gave and the man was sucked underneath. Thankfully, the agony muffled by the thing's weight upon head and chest.

"Back, move back," he shouted as the two other Ghosts were released when burning moss hit home, red welts upon their abdomens. Moving as a group, they swept side to side to keep the smaller Boush back, with the larger one busy feeding. They held them at bay for now. Radio signals then came in thick and fast from volunteers and soldiers, describing the movement of the Boush as they formed their ravenous colonies, the quicker, larger, and more aggressive form.

Swooping over their heads, a roar of engines startled the Ghost convoy as they set eyes on the blue metalled spaceship for the first time, ducking instinctively with the fire of the engines so close. It rotated in the air, landing across the road in front of the children, their panic rising in response to their blocked escape path.

Rear doors swung open, a beckoning figure and a loud voice barking through the Ghosts' radio, "Here, in here now."

"You heard her, everyone in. Adults turn and block the Boush, children in first. Keep them back," shouted Wendyll in the radio, in the air, to the wind. He swung round as the large Boush finished its meal, riding its wavelike movements to surge towards him as they defended the rear. Ghost soldiers slipped in beside them, the rifles discarded, fistfuls of roots bound together forming a blaze of light and heat. Wendyll took one of the proffered stacks, sweeping it in front as the Boush pushed them inwards.

Just another two minutes, nearly there.

Assailed from three sides by the ever-growing Boush, the mix of teachers, soldiers and volunteers swept the moss sticks around them, prodding and feinting at the molds in a desperate attempt to keep them back. Suddenly the slime molds changed tactics, shooting out pseudopods and wrapping tendrils around calves and ankles, pulling and yanking their prey to the floor, dragging them towards a slime filled doom. The army of humanity struck back, stabbing at the sucking appendages, burning through the thinner sections and releasing most of the fallen. Cries of fear and pain rang out, soon muffled as slime engulfed them.

"Now Wendyll, the children are in. Bring the rest with you." Wendyll responded to the cry from his second-in-command, ushering his people back, taking one step at a time, never turning their backs in fear of the lash of a tendril.

Wendyll called names, sending four running back to the ship, then another four leaving him with Mander, Threll and a soldier he didn't know. They swept the last few steps, keeping the monsters at bay.

"Now, it's got to be now. We need to shut the door," came the cry from the unknown saviour.

"Go," commanded Wendyll, his voice offering no recourse and the last three threw their torches down in front of him and ran. Wendyll drew out a sigh, a release. He'd done his job.

If only Reya could have held my hand under the night sky and kissed me one last time.

Tendrils whipped out, lashing at his body, ravenous and keen for blood. Wendyll closed his eyes, not wanting to eye the death that awaited, as the whip like cords wrapped around him and pulled.

Backwards.

He landed at Yasuko's feet, the last of the nanobots fading with energy depletion, the cord loop dissipating as the doors closed on the monsters without.

"You do not die this day," Yasuko whispered as she faded away, spent.

CHAPTER 43

Seth City

Kinsik scanned the maelstrom of yellow and green that pulsed amongst the vehicles surrounding the hospital. Having surveyed the car park and exits in that direction, Hander remained convinced going through was the best way. The children were weak, with nightfall due soon and an already darkening sky.

Kinsik fretted.

"Another Phalanx is on the way. Sfendonatai Cremal's clearance team, about thirty minutes. What now, Lance Corporal Zuberi?" said Hander.

"I say we wait until they arrive, clear the route with the medicinal alcohol incendiaries and get the children back to the temple. It's going to be dark soon. You can see the children back."

"You're not coming?"

"That depends. Can I borrow your ex-firefighter? Could do with her skillset."

"Lendrick? Ah, yes, now I see. I think she'd like to help."

Zuri grimly smiled in response. "Take Kinsik for me. Keep her safe. I made a promise to someone I aim to keep."

"I'm staying with you. Whatever you're planning, I can help," butted in the indignant Ghost.

"You have done enough; we'll be with you soon. Maybe even before you go. Stay with Hander and his Phalanx." Zuri's tone waylaid any complaint. Kinsik had learnt that much in the last few days, and with body sagging, she nodded agreement.

"Noah, with me. And Lendrick, fancy some payback?"

"Very much so," said Lendrick as they walked back to the hospital.

"What are they doing, Hander? What's so important?" Kinsik asked.

"I think they are planning a little firework party for the Boush. That storeroom looked very tempting. Boom." Hander mimed an explosion, cracking his first smile since they reached the hospital.

Twenty minutes later, Kinsik caught sight of the relief Phalanx on the other side of the tanker created corridor. Hander was talking rapidly into his radio, and she felt the tension rise as they prepared a plan.

Are they planning on leaving Noah and Zuri behind?

"Zuri, will you be long?" Kinsik spoke to her radio.

"No," came a muffled reply, "ten minutes. Is the other Phalanx there?"

"Yes, I'll let Hander know. Just ten?"

"Yes, we are just setting a trail through the corridor."

Trail?

"Hander!" shouted Kinsik. "They are nearly here. Can we delay for ten minutes?"

Hander signalled wait, while speaking into his radio.

"No more than five, Kinsik. They are fending off attacks from behind." She relayed the message, but Zuri was set on completing the job.

Still anxious, the young Ghost wandered to the doors of the hospital, desperate to urge her new friends on. Glancing through the doors, she saw them at work, busy in the increasing gloom, setting things out on the floor and pouring liquid over them.

Maybe a fire trail?

"Hurry, we are leaving," she urged over the radio.

"Go, we have more incendiaries. You want to help, stay with Hander. If I know you are safe, I will make better and quicker choices. Understand?" said Zuri.

"Yes." Reluctantly, Kinsik returned to Hander, feeling low and useless.

Why can't I help? It'd be quicker.

"Kinsik," said Hander, "with me now, please. Stay near, it is time to go." Hander lit the first of the medicinal bottles, throwing towards the near part of the corridor. Another swiftly followed from his squad, a third just beyond that. With the small Boush burnt or oozing towards cover, they moved cautiously out as the flames lowered.

"Smith, Lendrick, have they gone?" asked Zuri as she spread the blood bag over the floor. Lendrick, watching through the door, gave the thumbs up.

"On their way, looks like the other Phalanx is under stress from the rear. Better get moving."

"Noah, let's get this finished."

Noah heaved the grim trolley out the doors, laying the human remains he'd found as a trail, with Zuri using the last of the blood bags behind him. Not pleasant work, but Zuri was adamant they needed some payback, and if he was honest, he felt desensitised from it all. This mold had not chosen humans as a food source, it had simply landed with a drive to feed and reproduce like all life. Revenge wasn't important, saving more lives was, and the less Boush there were, then the more people survived.

Once finished, they couldn't help but quickly clean their hands before speeding out the door as Hander's Phalanx and the tired children reached halfway. With Zuri at the front and Noah taking the rear, they ran into the fray. Their *weapons* keeping the encroaching Boush at bay as they joined the back of the group, relieved to be keeping the children safe. Noah and Zuri took the rear, their return greeted by Kinsik with relief.

On making it to the end of the seething mass of metal and Boush, Hander's squad greeted Cremal, handing out more of the newly made Molotov cocktails from their backpacks. Zuri and Noah eyed the hospital, using their rifle sights to note the sudden surge of Boush heading in through the doors. Noah gave a curt nod back to Zuri and Lendrick, before moving back towards the Temple, and hopefully out of the nightmare city.

CHAPTER 44

Ruthyl

Finn clambered into the vibrating helicopter, the unfamiliar feel of the helmet a reminder of Zuri, the image of her wearing his, with Smith attached, flickering through his mind. He savoured it for a second, a smile playing across his lips. The dual blades spun up to speed, matching the twin tail rotors, and balancing the craft as they lifted off. Finn signalled out of the cockpit window as they hovered, ensuring the team below attached the enclosed bucket and hosing, tangle free. They were about to trial the first of the heli-torches, the ground test having proved that the engineers of Ruthyl were good at their jobs, and the Assistant Prime good for her word. Ready, the machine rose into the air, and they headed off north. If you were going to test something, you may as well try it where it would have most effect, despite the fading light.

After thirty minutes, they met the caravan of vehicles that marked the refugees from Seth, now supported by Ruthyl soldiers with their armoured vehicles, flanking both sides. Stremall explained on the way that the armoured cars and tanks were death-traps, too many vents and ways for Boush to enter. The New Halton heavy armour had rapidly been overwhelmed, next to useless. The Hoplite hadn't said it, but Finn was sure over-confidence may have been a factor. Stremall had already explained all this to the Ruthyl engineers, and their adaptions were being prepared as they spoke. Another weapon to their armoury once completed, and again Finn was grateful to Tethin for the belief and political will to back them up. That woman had saved more lives than anyone in Ruthyl, even before they encountered the Boush.

As the light faded, Finn gaped at the Boush horde appearing on the horizon. Twenty or more of the huge mounds rippled and surged towards them as they flowed alongside the road. With each pulsing wave, they ripped up the vegetation underneath, eating as they chased the rich protein escaping ahead. Coming up on them, Finn saw more behind the lead group, smaller, slower but still a formidable force to be reckoned with, and if they merged, well... Finn shuddered.

"Sweep to the right and we'll release above the fields first, see if we can move some on," said Finn over the radio, Pedon Fayde responding as she moved the helicopter and its load across the highway. Once out to the flank, Finn checked on the soldier in the hold, his fingers on the release and ignition buttons.

"Now," he said, acting as the spotter. The thickened aviation fuel released, with the spark from the ignition setting it alight. The stream of fiery liquid poured from the tank, and the field erupted with angry flames. Despite the tight timeline Finn had set them, the Ruthyl engineers had come through.

So far so good.

"Off," he said. The soldier responded, shutting the valve with a sigh of relief as Finn gave them the thumbs up. It was more than likely they'd be dumping the fuel all in one go, but the shut off was a much-needed fail-safe if the helicopter got into difficulties. Hoplite Stremall slapped the soldier on the back, the pleased look on her face suggesting that Finn's replacement for her proposed helicopter mounted flamethrower was an effective option, and much safer.

"Let's burn some Boush," she said over the radio. Finn felt the darkness pressing in, knowing this moment would come. Right now, he couldn't risk being hands on, and the smoke and flame would be another painful layer on top of the memories the Boush brought with them. His thigh tremored slightly. Finn pressed a hand down hard upon it, blocking out his thoughts with pain.

"You spot, Stremall," he said, offering his seat to the Hoplite, who gladly accepted. Finn took her seat; it was enough to know that the idea worked. He tried to focus on how Zuri was doing, and whether Yasuko had made it to the mines. But the smell of a melting boot and flesh kept creeping into his mind, and he felt the ghost of fear tickle at his anxiety. Finn pressed his hand harder into the wounded thigh, the pain washing everything away.

CHAPTER 45

Yasuko's Ship, Outside Of The Seth Foothills, Northern Road To New Halton

Wendyll stared at the spaceship's blue-hued ceiling, his heart still pounding despite being at rest for the past hour. Next to him, the children played ring games as the teachers took charge, the ship completely unresponsive and unmoving. They needed to distract the children from all the strangeness and possible trauma of the last hour. The other adults milled around or fed their babies, tended wounds, and mourned their losses despite the suffering being so much less than they thought before the ship took them in.

Wendyll eased himself up, attaining a sitting position that his aching muscles demanded, with the relief in his back also welcome.

"I am Yasuko," came the whisper near to his ear. Looking to his left, a faint image appeared, flat and unmoving, the pilot he'd seen on the King's screen. "I am at minimal power, used up. I can provide protection; the Boush cannot get through the hull, and I am recycling the air. I have water, but there's little food, I'm afraid."

Despite her sudden appearance, Wendyll soon came to terms with being so close to his faded saviour.

"The protection is enough, I—"

"No need for gratitude, Wendyll of the Ghosts Within. I help as it is what I can do. The emotions feel more comfortable than those of destruction and control. The New Halton soldiers are not far, about ten minutes away. They know where you are."

"Is there anything we can do? Fetch fuel or?"

"No… well yes. Tell me what you know about the Boush. I have observed their behaviour in this form, and their rapid change to the ravenous colonies, but do you know more? Tell me of their history so I may know better the reasons they hunt as they do."

Wendyll nodded, concern and apprehension for his people etched over his face. But this ship and Yasuko had been their salvation, and the price was not high. So he talked.

CHAPTER 46

Seth City

"The way has been cleared," said Hoplite Steen. "I know it's nightfall, but I say we go now."

"We're strung out, Hoplite, and the rescued children are weak. You have enough food and water now for another night, and a bit more time may mean the New Halton soldiers are closer when we get past the walls. I would say a morning reccy of the route followed by a run for the walls. It would give us the best chance."

Steen contemplated Zuri's words, chin in hand and eyes searching for Cremal to respond.

"I agree, Hoplite. Better to be rested, we know what's out there and the more light we have, the safer we will be." Steen listened, and then stood, eyes roaming over the people under his protection.

"We go in the morning, pack now and rest well," Steen's words echoed around the vaulted ceiling. The hubbub within the room dropped and then rose again in anxious excitement.

"I hope—" An enormous eruption vibrated through the stone walls, cutting Steen short. The whole temple fell silent once again until Hander and his soldiers moved amongst them, explaining the blast to resounding slaps on their backs.

"And that," said Zuri with satisfaction, "means a few less Boush to worry about." She walked over and gave Lendrick a gentle hug, avoiding the reset broken arm at her side, and gripped Noah's shoulder as she went by.

"So why send me away?" asked Kinsik, for the eighth or ninth time. Noah's battered restraint edging towards an angry retort before Zuri stepped in.

"Because I said so, Kinsik, and sometimes that is enough," said Zuri. Noah gave her a grateful smile. The girl huffed and stormed off, the first real sign of the teenager within that they'd seen for a while. "That's a good sign, Noah, a normal reaction amongst all of this chaos. You okay?" She could see he wasn't.

Mchimba kisima huingia mwenyewe. He who digs a pit will fall into it himself. Ah, my pit, I should never have dragged you into the hospital, Noah. I am sorry.

"You mean apart from..." he trailed off, the response a waste of emotion. Noah sat on the floor, head between his legs as his stomach tied itself in knots. Maybe not so desensitised as he thought. Zuri knelt down, wrapping her arms around the man who'd been a rookie only a little over a month ago. Angry at herself, she should have just walked away. Revenge can be bitter.

"I'm sorry, Noah. I should not have made you do it. I had to do something, after... after it grabbed me, the fear would not pass. I needed to strike back, but should have found another way, asked Hander maybe." Zuri leant her head into Noah, "I am so sorry."

"It's okay, I'm not even sure it was that," he said through the welling of emotion. "It's just been relentless. Is this what we are now?"

"Would you have changed it? The lives we have saved? Do we ignore those people, could we accept more death if we have the power to do something about it? To me, Yasuko and the ship are a gift. I can make a difference where I tread. But I am prone to emotions that cloud my judgement, Noah, and until we return to Earth, maybe I need your conscience to keep me in check. Be that voice, and if you choose not to act, there'll be no judgement from me."

"Just a little lie, he won't notice," said Smith, just to Zuri.

Noah looked up, his red-rimmed eyes and slight smile sending a clear message.

"Ah, maybe he will."

"Finn, Zuri, Smith, Noah, can you hear me?" Yasuko's voice echoed over their radios, weak but defined enough to hear.

"Yes," they all said in unison, Finn and Zuri awash with relief at hearing each other's distant voices.

"I have someone called Wendyll and his Ghosts on the ship. Wendyll told me about a fifth stage of the Boush. They form a hardened mound with a central bulge. It should be the final sporing stage."

"What? We get even more of those things? It's bad enough as it is."

"No, I think it's related to the cosmic dust cloud. Its trailing edge is due to pass in the next five to six days and the light from Bathsen's suns is already increasing as it thins. That's why they're in a feeding frenzy. The light is their trigger to spore."

"But it still means there will be more of them. We need to burn as many as we can."

"I think it's better news than that. Their spores came from space, right? From the cosmic dust—"

"Ah," said Noah, the information clicking into place, "They spore to reach space, so their final stage needs to fire spores up into the atmosphere. Some will eventually join the dust cloud and wait for the next planetfall. If we fend them off until they harden and become immobile, the Boush will spore and die, and the planet will be mainly free. Or at least, in theory."

"That's what I was thinking. Defend Ruthyl, Finn, and then stop them reaching the other cities. Buy some time. I suspect they will have to achieve a critical mass before they can spore, so there'll be an urge to join up. That will be our signal to back off," said Yasuko, her voice petering away.

"I'm trying, and Stremall too. Zuri, I'm okay. Helping with planning a defence, no combat on Yasuko's orders. Stay safe," said Finn, the words spilling out in a rush.

"And you, *mpenzi wangu*," she replied, hands against her chest, trying to hold herself in.

"I am fading. I've cannibalised some mass to manage this message. I wish you well." Yasuko ended her call, leaving them all, including Finn and Zuri, disconnected once again.

"What we don't know is what happens to those Boush that don't attain the right mass for sporing. But we should have the time to deal with that afterwards," said Noah, though Zuri was lost in thought and not listening. "Hopefully with science and not the gun."

CHAPTER 47

Yasuko's Ship, Outside Of The Seth Foothills, Northern Road To New Halton

Wendyll jumped in the armoured carrier's rear, the wooden bench welcome after the metal of Yasuko's ship. He would never stop appreciating her gift of life for his people and himself, but the familiarity of the wood felt less otherworldly. Three of the Phalanxes remained with the children, waiting for dawn before using their commandeered vehicles to ensure the children reached New Halton safely.

Wendyll's focus switched to returning to Reya, travelling with the remaining Sfendonatai as they headed to his adopted home. The attached trailer contained their flamethrowers and spare fuel, much welcomed resources as they sought to defend the City Within from the hated Boush. The final three Akontistai reserve Phalanxes remained behind, waiting for morning inside the ship, facing a march through Boush infested territory to meet up with Wendyll in the Ghost's city.

And now we make sacrifices for each other, when for so long we could barely look each other in the eye.

How the world had changed, with spaceships and a war of attrition against creatures arriving via cosmic dust. Wendyll did not know where it would end, but needed Reya and Kinsik to be in his arms when it did. With thoughts of the beautiful Gallery wafting through his mind, sleep finally took him.

◆ ◆ ◆

Wendyll woke up as the armoured carrier jerked to a stop, the Hoplite giving a reassuring grin before exiting the vehicle into the morning light. As Wendyll joined him, he could sense the change in the air. Not only was the wet season turning, but the dust was also thinning. This was a morning of old, the dual suns' light bouncing off the morning clouds. Wendyll looked to the show cave. They must have wound their way through much of the rocks and debris with the huge-wheeled vehicle bouncing its way to within half a kilometre.

How did I sleep through that?

The Phalanx swiftly unloaded. Clearly thinking ahead, they'd brought heavy duty trolleys with them as they shifted their equipment towards the cave entrance, two Sfendonatai always on guard. Wendyll activated his radio beacon, this entrance to his city no longer a secret, but still difficult to enter from the outside. The response pulse came back, and the door glided open, a young teenage boy beckoning them in, not one Wendyll recognised.

"How goes it?" he asked, standing aside as the soldiers wheeled the fuel inside.

"An hourly battle. They seem never-ending and move about the air ducts at will. We have lost many, though the New Halton's stand beside us, exhausted and low on fuel as they are. You are a welcome sight, Wendyll. Reya asked to see you immediately."

"I will send the vehicle back for another Phalanx. It'll leave us one short, but if the lad's right, then we need more soldiers," said the Hoplite.

"Here." Wendyll handed over the transmitter to the Hoplite. "Get them to use this and we'll let them in. I can't risk it being left open as another Boush entrance." With that, he turned and led the remaining soldiers down towards his beloved Gallery. The young lad, whose name he kicked himself for not asking, stayed behind.

He set the pace high; the soldiers recognising his need for urgency and keeping the trolleys moving, grateful to see another set waiting near the entrance for the next Phalanx. Wendyll led them through the maze of carved corridors, taking the direct route with time of the essence, and all concern over strangers lost amongst the need for aid.

They reached the doorway and were quickly inside to be greeted by the smell of burning fuel and moss. The upper gallery was full of wounded and crying people, Ghosts driven from their homes, their coloured clothing torn and seared from the Boush's attacks. As the new soldiers entered, the Ghosts greeted them with waves and tired smiles, coupled with looks of desperate thanks.

"Gear up my Sfendonatai. We have work to do. Wendyll, do we have anyone that can stand with us to guard against the hidden ones?" said the Hoplite.

"We will," said Reya, striding into the gallery alongside a group of grubby Ghosts, smelling of smoke and fire with moss torches in their hands. She took Wendyll in her arms. "Tell me they are safe?"

"We lost Talik, and a few more whose names I've lost in the rush. But the children are safe, the New Halton's are seeing them to their city. I returned with these, and there are more on the way." Wendyll stepped back, sensing the tremble in Reya. "You have not slept. You're exhausted my love. It is time to let others step in."

"I—"

"Time for all of us," came the cry from the back, an old man stepping forwards. "Rest Reya. Wendyll will lead and the Ghosts Within will take the strain. Who's with me?" shouted the man, with others standing to his cry. "We have enough, Reya. Your team needs to rest so you can be ready for when we tire."

"Thank you, dad," said Reya. "But—"

"Rest. Come, Wendyll. Let's see how best we can serve."

CHAPTER 48

Ruthyl

Finn sat in the expansive meeting room; the fine wooden table polished to a sheen with beautifully carved chairs underneath. It meant so little to him, the trappings of power and wealth, when those beneath the boot remained excluded. Before him, Prime Brenan sat with the leaders of the three southern cities down by the coast. Each had their own worries, mainly because of the lack of city walls. They all wanted to see how Ruthyl planned to defend themselves. What Finn needed, and the three other people in the room agreed with, were their helicopters, aviation fuel and cooperation with what came afterwards.

"Lance Corporal Finn," started Assistant Prime Tethin, "could you explain your plan for all the leaders with Strategos Hoskan."

Finn stood, the Strategos by his side adding gravity to his presence. The man was a peacetime general, a manager of scant resources, like most of the cities. Why bother when there were no threats and land was plentiful?

"The walls are low, but the adapted flamethrowers will defend the north, east and western sections. The walls are also long, and the Strategos has staged the throwers specifically where the moat has weak points. With time we would have dug through the rock, but needs must. Once the Boush gather, we will pour the fuel down the walls and towards the moat, setting it alight." Finn stood aside, Hoplite Stremall joining them.

"The Boush can push on through fire, sacrificing some of the colony to get over the walls. That's why your adapted system allows us to aim downwards between them and the wall, peeling them off with fire. We didn't have a moat at New Halton, but once that's alight, the Boush on the walls will have nowhere else to go but over. It needs to be timed well, or their desperation will overrun the positions. They may split, at which point they slow down and swarm. A single house-sized Boush can have four or five hundred smaller ones, possibly more. I suggest mobile flamethrower teams on the wall who can intercept, a luxury we did not have." Stremall sat down. Unused to talking with powerful figureheads she was relieved to have got through her piece.

"Any questions on defence?" asked Strategos Hoskan.

"No," replied Prime Brenan, "all seems in hand. I have arranged for as many of the citizens as we can to be on the lake. The weather forecast looks good, calm, so we can minimise the people inside should the worst happen, and that'll give the Sfendonatai space to operate should they be needed. Now, Lance Corporal, explain your plans for before they arrive. You are looking to reduce their numbers considerably, if possible."

Finn looked at the leaders. This was a cause they needed to get behind. "We plan to use the three helicopters Ruthyl has to torch the Boush out in the fields. Hoplite Stremall came up with the idea of fire from above, and with the engineers you have, it proved relatively easy. That," said Finn, eyeing the group, "is what you need to be doing right now. Take the design and build your own. You have hundreds of Boush heading your way, bypassing Ruthyl. Harry them, delay them, and if we survive the day, we can chase them down from behind. Thin them out before they reach your cities, help each other defend and you stand a chance. Once they pass us, they won't come back. You have started the town clearances, but that'll need to speed up as my ship has reached its limits. It's down to you." Finn sat down, maintaining his outward professional demeanour as his inner darkness pressed in with the rising anxiety. Tiredness still ached in his bones and leg, but Yasuko had been right. This was going to save lives.

"Thank you all," said Brenan, dismissing them while turning to the other leaders. Finn knew there'd be a scheme underneath their discussions, some way of profiting. Nevertheless, Brennan had heard them out under the steady gaze of the Assistant Prime. There appeared to be no refusal of the plan.

"Strategos, Finn, might I have a word?" asked Stremall. "I have another idea."

CHAPTER 49

Seth City

Sfendonatai Cremal returned with her Phalanx, one soldier down after a Boush ambush near the main city gates. The middle-sized slime mold had exploded from underneath a vehicle, its tendril pulling a soldier under the car before anyone could react. It had been their first loss since emerging from the Temple, but sorely felt, souring Hoplite Steen's mood. To his mind, everyone was his responsibility and with the citizens swollen to nearly fifteen hundred, he aimed to get each one to safety.

"Lance Corporal Zuri, can you and your team go ahead? Secure the gates, keep them free while my Sfendonatai bring the people through. If I know we have safe passage at the gates, then if we need to make a break for it, we can." The Hoplite had already discussed splitting the survivors into smaller groups, but dismissed the idea as he worked through the number of soldiers he'd need. Whatever way you looked at it, they were short. The Hoplite stopped, caught by Kinsik's actions as she walked amongst the children, painting symbols on their cheeks.

"What's she doing, Zuri?" he asked, the sour mood adding a bitter tone to his words.

"The large Boush chased Kinsik—"

"Acted as bait, you mean," interrupted the girl.

"—And she fell amongst its slime, the clear stuff they travel on. It wouldn't go near her and appeared confused enough that we could destroy it." Kinsik nodded during Zuri's recounting. "Cremal's brought back this slime for her. It may well be the key to keeping the kids safe, so why not?"

Kinsik had mixed the last of her stone powder in the slime and drawn on the children, telling them they were the Ghosts Within protective symbols. The older children pretended to accept the marks as an example to the youngest, but Kinsik sensed a need for something to hold on to.

"It won't harm them. The only effect on Kinsik was to turn her into an extra grouchy teenager," said Zuri, waiting for the reaction.

The teenage Ghost whipped round, the stare withering, to be greeted by Zuri's smug smile. Kinsik carried on drawing over the children, angry but proud at the same time. Zuri had approved of what she was doing, in a backhanded way at least. She finished by using the little left on her own boots. Couldn't harm if they struck out low.

"It's clear out there, Zuri. Sun's up over the wall, reducing the shadows. Time for us to move," said Smith

Packing one each of the hospital bottle bombs, the three of them set off, with Zuri's battered armour in Kinsik's eyeline as she took point, Noah at the rear. They walked slowly through the street where they had defeated the huge Boush, the dried pieces splattered walls and the remaining windows. Kinsik kept Zuri's sidearm handy, the heavy rifle strapped to her back being less useful against the Boush, large or small.

"I have movement under the cars ahead, to the left. Small, possibly two of them."

Zuri crouched down, eyes along the ground, and she caught sight of the feeding mold. Two energy bolts released, and she carried on by the shrivelled Boush, their innards oozing onto the floor. In the warm sunlight they carried on along the street, Smith keeping them informed, and between them, six more of the Boush were no longer a threat.

"*You thinking what I'm thinking, Zuri?*"

"Give me a clue, Smith."

"*There's a lot of people back there, and I'm the one that can see them through. In this light, with my sensors, well...*"

"You could have thought of that beforehand, you know, like back there."

"*And tell them that a talking helmet was keeping them safe. I'm sure they'd listen.*"

"How about we secure the gates, then decide? If we are under attack there, then it may be best you stay."

"*Good point, deal. Turn here, we come out in fifteen metres at the main street. It's a right and then straight for four hundred metres to the gates. Nothing in this alley, at least nothing not shielded, but don't forget to look up.*"

"Funny, Smith. It was just the once."

"*Yeah, but the squelch when it landed was dis-gus-ting.*"

"Now I know why Finn wanted to hand you over. Keep this up and you're going in the slime."

Zuri led them through the alley, eyes roaming across the upturned boxes and bins as they made their way. The tighter spaces always felt worse, and the smashed windows above didn't help. Once at the alley exit, Smith gave them the 'all clear' for the first fifty metres.

"Kinsik, keep close," said Zuri, surveying the wide road cluttered with abandoned vehicles. "Cremal lost a soldier to some bigger Boush out here, watch the windows and underneath the cars. The suns are strong, but they're getting bolder."

"Okay, Zuri."

Noah swept the area behind, only the swing of car doors

clattering broke the silence. It felt eery after the frantic behaviour back at the hospital. The atmosphere was heavy, and the hairs on his arms and neck rose. He kept sweeping below the cars, dread creeping in on him unannounced.

It looks picked clean. But something's here.

His eyes roamed towards Zuri, her rifle at her chin as she stepped forward, constantly surveying. She felt it too, her steps becoming more and more measured. But Smith was silent, no words of warning.

The car exploded upwards, flung into the air and spinning wildly to slam onto the other side of the street. Underneath, Cremal's soldier reaching out, her legs stuck solid amongst the hardening Boush beneath, mouth wide in a silent scream, eyes beseeching. The Boush's huge pseudopod pulsed with power as it writhed, almost fighting itself as the hardening crust crept up its outer layer.

Kinsik hit the floor, instincts making her duck the flying metal with the squirming tentacle driving towards her. Rolling, she grabbed a car door, wrenching it open to block the attack. Zuri's energy bolts seared into the tendril, cutting off the last metre before she raked up its length. Noah dived towards Kinsik, grabbing under her arms and yanking her away as the Boush speared another pseudopod on its ravenous way. It grabbed at her feet, recoiling as it tasted the slime, then redirected the assault at Noah. An explosion of flame erupted on the green blob's surface, Zuri's tossed bottle bursting with fire, forcing the tentacle to retract in swirling pain.

As the flames took hold, Kinsik rose, her sidearm ready, pointing towards the burning soldier. Noah pushed it down, shaking his head and looking to his current squad commander. Zuri took careful aim, taking the shot to end the soldier's agony. She turned towards them both, her eyes full of the horror, and the necessity. The flames licked at the soldier's body; its fresh wound soon consumed by fire.

"Zuri, that Boush was the same ambient temperature. No way to pick it up. Sorry. And that was necessary, no way to save her."

"See if you can find a way, Smith. They're not mobile in that form, but if undetected we will lose people," she replied, aching, heartfelt pain tempering her words.

No life lessons here. Move on. Me and mine are still safe, we survive.

Noah walked over, taking point as he gave Zuri the nod to move back for a while. She looked at him closely; it was exactly what Finn would do. Move the distressed soldier out of the firing line, prevent the mistake. She nodded, moving to the back.

"Nearly there," she said to Kinsik on the way past, "and you don't need that in your dreams every night. It's what we do. But anyone who is prepared to make that choice, who could do that for another? Even if they're a teenager, I call them deserving of respect."

Heat hit Kinsik's cheeks, the covering of stone dust thankfully hiding it from Zuri.

CHAPTER 50

Ruthyl

Stremall packed the last of the detonators in the pickup's cab, down amongst the phosphorus and cans of fuel. Finn watched on, annoyed she'd stopped him from helping, but admiring her steadfast refusal to take any of his crap.

I feel so much safer now that's in place. Not.

Finn patted her on the back, sweaty from the exertion of carrying the cans that packed the rear. Around them, an assortment of cars and trucks littered the front of Ruthyl's moat, the last road in currently being reduced to a single lane after the latest group of refugees arrived. Soon it would be time for even that to go. Time to batten down, ready for the rush of gelatinous death heading their way. Any more arrivals would need to hail the boats waiting near the small docking bay on the eastern side.

Finn had to admire the ingenuity of the Ruthyl people. If they, and the other cities, had paid heed to the warnings from Jonkren, they could have worked together and saved many more people. They lacked the trust and imagination required, Stremall's wild ideas putting them to shame. Though there were now more signs of hope for the future. The new pontoon landing pads on the lake for the lighter helicopters used by the southern cities, had created space on Ruthyl's helipads, and widened the reach of the heli-torch idea. An indication that cooperation and ingenuity were finally working hand in hand.

Stremall gave him a last handshake. "I'm not going to enjoy

the journey there amongst the offal and fuel. It smells dreadful already."

"I don't envy you, not a great combination. Are you sure this going to work?"

"Worth a try," she said. "What do we lose? A few vehicles and some fuel. Take a few out and our chances improve."

"The helicopters will follow a few minutes behind. Be careful, I think the cities are going to need that wild brain of yours again before this is over." Stremall returned a pained grin, head down and kicking at the soil.

"It's the thought of my Sfendonatai, those I burnt upon the wall. It keeps me going. No one needs to go through that again, least of all me. I have sworn I will do all I can, and you need to do the same, Finn. I heard you in the night crying out, pacing the room. The guards were knocking on my door asking if there's anything we can do. Whatever tortures your soul, you have to find a way to deal with it rather than bottling it up. It will eat you alive more surely than the Boush."

Sucking his lips into a soured smile, Finn replied, "I know. My centre is Zuri. When she's around, things are easier but..." Finn looked to the sky, holding it in. "Nights are difficult. Everything comes flooding back, whether they're real or not. My dreams well... let's just say it's better to be awake."

Stremall nodding, said, "Yes, the dreams I can relate to. Everything is vivid, even the smell," she closed her eyes, nostrils flaring, "I regret bringing it up now." Tears pooled at the corner of her eyes. Finn stumbled over what to do next and chose a little awkward humanity, grabbing the Hoplite's shoulder and squeezing.

"See, talking isn't easy. Let's do a deal. You get through this and we'll both open up." The Hoplite squeezed Finn's hand upon her shoulder and entered the cab.

"You'd better be there then. Don't be late." Stremall started her engine, the signal for the convoy of twenty vehicles to form up. Finn hobbled to the waiting Ruthyl helicopters, its rotors already spinning as the urgency took hold. Rising into the air, the southern city helicopters joined them as they followed the Hoplite's crazy idea up the road, towards the Boush.

"They are on approach, Stremall. You need to form up as soon as possible and get your arses out of there," said Finn over the radio, the helicopter hovering thirty metres above the fuel-laden convoy.

"On it."

Finn scanned the horizon, his trusty monocular to his eye and rifle across his lap. There must have been thirty of the house-sized molds now pulsating along and beside the road, three or four deep in places. Yasuko had talked of them communicating, and watching them now gave a sense of order and rank, keeping to their own path. At the rate they travelled, Ruthyl needed to be prepared for a dawn arrival, and he needed scouts in place along the route in case they upped the pace. Sighing, he watched as Stremall organised the vehicles across the road and just about in the path of the oozing wave.

"Need to spread out a little, about five metres more on each flank. These things are keeping to a straight line. You need to be wider to make sure you're in the way."

Stremall moved the cars out in response to Finn's guidance, with ten in front and the others filling the gaps in a second row behind.

"Time to move, Stremall, so bring your drivers in," Finn said, signalling the Pedon to take them down.

The helicopters all took turns to land, experienced pilots keeping the spread of rotors and down draft absolutely safe. As Stremall and five others reached Finn's, she gave the thumbs up, and they took flight. The pilots kept their holding pattern in range for the detonators, but far enough away to prevent the explosions and heated updrafts from causing issues.

"Swap places, Stremall. You need a bird's-eye view to time your detonator."

And the last thing I need is smoke and flame right now.

Stremall's sweaty hands gripped the radio detonator. Needing to resist the urge to go too quick, she kept her finger hovering away from the safety switch, never mind the button underneath, with a determined focus on the marauding creatures seeping across the fields.

When the first Boush flowed over her truck, she kept her finger clear. As its tentacles slid through the windows hungrily searching for the offal within, she tapped at the release button, but still resisted.

Wait, breathe and wait.

Keeping her mind clear, she watched the other lead creatures' rippling bodies engulf the cars ahead: ten cars, ten house-sized pulsating masses feeding. Her eyes roamed to those at the back. With little space between the feeding Boush, she felt a change in those at the rear. They seemed to elongate and thin out, stretching between the feasting colonies, and yearning for the meat in the cars beyond.

"Hold," she ordered down the radio. "On my mark, 3—2—1, now." The vehicles erupted simultaneously, fire rushing under and upwards, ripping the huge Boush apart as fuel and flame spread. Ash-stained Boush split, the smaller forms sliding away from their shared grip, fleeing the flames. Those behind slid sideways, moving away from the heat, though tentative in their movements as they crossed each other's path, arching their co-joined bodies to ooze above the wet slime of their compatriots.

With the pilot circling, Finn could see the smaller Boush reforming through the side door, merging again into a new colony, a new house-sized Boush. Where there had been twenty huge slime molds ripped apart by fire, there now slid ten new ones, with ten more behind finding a path to join them from the rear.

"That's going to help, Stremall. You've cut their numbers by a third. Not bad for a crazy plan. If we'd had enough helicopters to bring the heli-torches as well, we could have doubled that. You people are really going to have to work together in the future. You'd be amazed at what you could achieve."

CHAPTER 51

City Within

Wendyll, back leant against the balustrade wall, pulled Reya in a little closer. The long, exhausting, night finally over. He was surrounded by the tired Ghosts who, collectively with the New Halton Phalanxes, had protected their home.

Overnight, the armoured vehicle had returned twice more, each load of fire toting soldiers adding weight to the battle for the City Within. At midnight the horde had reached its zenith, the creatures attempting to group up and colonise, leaving themselves briefly vulnerable, and the experienced soldiers laid down a withering assault. The burnt ash pervaded the Gallery, but the Boush had stopped coming. Who knows how many they would have lost with the children still in the city, the space and ferocity needed to end the siege could have led to disaster, and he was thankful of the considered decisions Reya, the Ghosts, and the King had made along the way.

But there was no time to rest, a debt owed needed to be repaid. Sliding Reya against her father's shoulder, he gave the man a nod before standing to stretch out his back. Wendyll checked with the Phalanx on guard. Reassured that all was well below, he left the Upper Gallery and walked on into the tunnels beyond. Finding himself alongside a young teenage boy he recognised, he had a chance at a little redemption.

"What's your name, lad?" he asked.

"Bandle, Sunik Bandle. But everyone calls me Ban," came the

detailed reply, the boy's tired face cracking in a worthy smile.

"Well Ban, are you okay to come with me to the surface? I could do with a little company, and that moss and root will make me feel a little safer."

Eagerly nodding, the teenager lifted the root to check the moss was firmly attached and then slipped in beside Wendyll as they travelled the tunnels.

"What do you think of the soldiers, Ban? You okay with them knowing about our home?"

The boy didn't respond immediately, the Ghost in him demanding careful thought before replying, "Without them I think we would have lost the city, and many of us. Whether or not we all agree, we need to accept it and make the best we can. A Ghost should be thankful of the beauty within, and maybe now the possibilities without."

Wendyll clapped the boy on the shoulder. "Can I use that, Ban? In a speech? I think you just summed up everything I was thinking."

"Really? My words?"

"Not just the words, Ban. Words have no meaning without the belief behind them. We have come so close to losing our home, and the other cities might well fall in the next few days. If we don't stand together, then all this may happen again. The 'possibilities without' are indeed the key to humanity's future."

When they finally made it to the show cave door, Wendyll opened it, carefully checking it was free from Boush. Asking Ban to wait, he departed, taking his usual place on the rock above the cave to radio New Halton. After a brief wait and a few repeated messages, he got through to the King.

"Wen, so pleased you are alive. And your city?"

"As good as can be, thanks to your soldiers, Your Majesty. The children, are they safe?"

"Yes, only just arrived, but they're inside the walls. The people rallied and sent civilian vehicles to fetch them back. I'm quite proud of my citizens, Wen. There may be some hope for us all yet."

"Can a thankful man ask for one more favour then?"

Wendyll rapped on the blue metal hull. No echo but a gentle blue pulsing light came in response. The door slid slowly open.

"Yasuko? You there?" he said.

"Yes, Wendyll, though most of my systems are dormant."

"Will this help?" Wendyll placed the heavy box on the floor, lifting the lid and rolling the chunk of palladium onto the airlock floor. Amazed, he watched the floor shimmer like a liquid metal sea before the lump was absorbed. After a few seconds, a glow emanated from the ceiling.

"Thank you, Wendyll. It'll definitely help."

"There's more outside. Where do you want it?"

Yasuko sent her sensors outward, the newly invigorated system picking up the New Halton hexacopter and the large bag of palladium it had dropped next to the ship. Enough to get her back to the mine and recover the rest of the mined ore.

"Th—"

"No need for gratitude, Yasuko. I help as it is what *I* can do." Wendyll opened his arms wide, palms out. "What we should *all* do; your example sets many people on this planet to shame."

CHAPTER 52

Seth City

They reached the gates with relative ease after their encounter with the hardening Boush, just a few of the smaller creatures to despatch along the way. What worried Zuri most was the closeness of the vehicles, bringing so many people through that tight space was a recipe for disaster. They'd seen the signs of Boush working together. Should they do so here, amongst the turmoil of cars and trucks, panic may set in, and they had few enough soldiers as it was. First, she needed the gateway clear, then the space beyond gates. After that, well, it was decision time on Smith's suggestion of going back, leaving only two to guard this end of the escape route.

"Noah, with me while we check the control room to the left. And Kinsik, watch our backs."

Noah stepped forward, taking the lead as per their silent agreement earlier. Zuri stretched her back, the chemically burnt skin chafing against the wrecked armour.

I need a shower, a Finn and a blue metal ship right now. In that order.

Noah approached the shattered doorway, peering in the side window. He felt confident it was clear, but procedure kept them alive.

"Are we clear Smith?" he asked.

"As a bell, whatever that means. No signature but there could be those crusty ones."

Using the mirror sight and switching to thermal as a double check, Noah confirmed his suspicions and stepped inside. Still keeping low, Zuri followed and together they swept the room, ignoring the closed door at the rear.

"Clear," Noah said, and they moved out to the second control room.

"I have a signature in there, at least one, possibly two small ones," said Smith.

In a similar state to the last room, Noah checked the space with his visor on thermal, picking up the colder signature of two Boush feeding against a broken table. Signalling to Zuri, he stepped through, sending energy bolts flying to sear through their outer membrane.

"Clear," he called after checking the rest of the space. "Are we calling this in?"

"No, I want those cars moving. I'd like a big space in front of the gates for a clear field of view and the same on the other side. Kinsik, you know how to get these vehicles moving?"

Kinsik shrugged, but moved over to the nearest one they'd already checked on the way in. Opening the door, and ignoring the smell, she worked her way through the controls, but soon concluded it was hopeless. Boats, yes, cars no. On a hunch she moved around the back, giving it a push, feeling the weight resist though there was a little give. Noah joined her, and as his hip and shoulder servos kicked in, they soon had it shifting.

"I think we should be able to get most moving at least a short distance," he said.

"No one puts the handbrake on when a mold the size of a house is after you."

Ten minutes of work, with Zuri on watch, got the area reasonably clear, and they moved to the front of the walls. Here the cars were in such disarray, nothing would make much of a difference. However, only dried slime and discarded clothing covered the paths at the side of the road. The bushes and trees ripped from the ground meant they had a clear view, with only the husks remaining strewn across the floor.

Beyond that, who knew? This was the northern gate. According to Yasuko, the huge Boush headed south on a feeding frenzy, meaning this was the safest way out. But Zuri had learned life the hard way, nothing was ever as it seemed, and that mistrust of things out of her control kept her alive.

Mwenda pole hajikwai. He who walks slowly does not stumble. Carefully does it.

"Zuri, are you there?" asked Yasuko over the radio.

Zuri broke into a smile, "Yes. Am I glad to hear from you. Are you able to help?"

"I have some capacity, but not a lot. I can make one run your way before returning to New Halton. That help?"

"A sensor sweep, and one pickup would be great. We have children in the city. Manage that?"

"Yes, I can do that. On my way. Be about twenty minutes, as I need to manage the engines carefully with such low fuel."

"Noah, call it in. Yasuko's on the way. ETA twenty minutes. You and Kinsik guard the gates while Smith and I move to the edge of the cleared area. Get Steen to call in when they reach the alleyway and I'll meet them there. And inform them about the hardening Boush, knowledge is power."

Zuri heard the rumble of Yasuko's engines before she caught welcome sight of the ship overhead. The glint of the twin suns off its blue hull lifted her spirits, but this was not the time to relax. Hope brought vulnerability, and that needed careful guarding.

"I have them, Zuri, and there's a couple of large Boush in pursuit. Hander is on the radio. His team are taking the rear guard for now, but they're out of the bottle bombs."

"Damn it, Smith, I left our last two bombs with Kinsik and Noah."

"For good reason, we need the exit clear. You know a bottleneck would be a disaster, like the one you're guarding now. This alleyway is vital. Stay on it and let the Phalanxes do their job."

Zuri forced herself to calm, working through each muscle group at a time, mirroring the gymnastic training routine she used to remove the anxiety of competition. Stiff muscles in her back resisted, but eventually gave in, and Zuri refocussed on the task ahead.

"Zuri, there are four Boush on the rooftop on either side of your position. Medium-sized but moving in, three to the left as you face and one to the right. Too close to your position for me to burn them, sorry. The way back through to the entrance remains clear of anything big enough for me to pick up. I'm setting down outside the walls now," said Yasuko.

"I've got them now, Zuri. Crap, two of them are merging."

"Tap into Steen's radio, inform him that the alleyway will need clearing first before they enter. Full info."

"Done. You need to watch your back. Your armour is compromised."

"Don't I know it. Keep reminding me, Smith. Need you to keep me alive."

"On it. I'll connect in with Steen. You can talk to him direct, and he'll understand."

Hoplite Steen came into view across the alley, signalling across to Zuri.

"Steen, we should be connected. The Boush are above and they must know you're coming. You got a plan?"

"Yeah, Hoplite bait. Coming down with a few volunteers to draw them out. We have the last three alcohol bombs and hopefully we can get out in time. They were ready for us, Lance Corporal. They must have followed the smell trail back to the Temple from the hospital rescue. These things..." Steen left it hanging. Zuri assumed there'd been more losses, time to put that at an end.

"I'll cover from this side, when you need me, call."

The Hoplite moved, slowly walking down the alleyway with his heavy rifle slung on his back. Behind, Zuri could see two Sfendonatai following, bottles in hand, similar to the Hoplite's.

"*The big ones on the move, coming over the edge,*" said Smith.

Zuri brought her rifle up, resisting the urge to fire, knowing they needed it further down and in effective range. It oozed above the edge, and she caught sight of the many appendages reaching out to drag the monstrous body over the apex. Slime dripped to ease its way, the creature shooting pseudopods to the far wall, steadying its pace as it slid inexorably downwards.

"*It's going to surge, going for the kill. Steen!*" bellowed Smith.

Zuri fired on instinct. Steen wasn't ready, misjudging the thing's speed. The energy bolts seared inwards to little effect, the huge bulbous mass rapidly dropping towards the Hoplite. Zuri stepped out from her cover, firing burst after burst, needing the Seth soldier to move.

"*Move Steen, run towards us. Run!*" shouted Smith.

The Boush released its grip on the wall, plummeting downwards as the Hoplite leapt forwards. Zuri's barrage continued; each burst absorbed by the ravenous mold as it landed on Steen's legs. He screamed, and the weight of the beast's hungry *regard* settled upon Zuri's shoulders.

"*Throw, now!*" shouted Smith.

Zuri surged forward, desperate, but knowing the scorching air was not enough, too low-powered when face to face with the quivering mass. The hot barrel dried out the Boush's outer edge, and she worked her way inwards, frantically trying to release Steen's legs as his agonised cries rang in her ears.

I need fire.

Zuri's elbow servos drove the muzzle deeper into the Boush when an unexpected eruption of flame shrivelled its flesh, the *weapon of choice* adapting to her demand. Bursts of liquid fire erupted, cooking the Boush flesh from the inside. More explosions followed, burnt ash flying as the Sfendonatai threw their Molotovs. The Boush whipped its tendrils upwards, attempting to flee. Removing the rifle-turned-flamethrower, Zuri pulled at Steen's shaking arms, dragging him from under the lifting creature and back towards the alley mouth.

"Zuri!"

She spun, twisting behind the bin at her side as tendrils lashed out, catching her exposed back. Ignoring the rising pain, she reached for her rifle, hearing the crash of broken glass as Steen threw. On the turn, she released liquid fire into the new Boush, igniting the alcohol from Steen's bottle and setting the Boush alight. Its medium-sized body quivered, the smaller Boush sliding apart, attempting to escape. Glancing over, and noting the two Sfendonatai driving the larger Boush upwards, she burnt the few that came near her or Steen's prone body.

"There's one left, but it's just absorbed one of the escaping molds. Zuri, it's turning away. These things communicate like Yasuko said."

Zuri dropped to Steen's side, hand on his wrist, seeking a pulse. The weak response gave hope, though it faded rapidly as she surveyed his ruined legs.

"Noah, Kinsik, they are on their way. Is the ship ready, Yasuko?"

"Yes, I'll open up when they arrive. Sensors show a clear run past the gates."

Zuri strode towards the Sfendonatai, instructing Smith to translate.

"Get them moving, now. We need everyone through this alleyway, immediately. Steen's alive, but barely. The people go first. It's what he'd want." The soldiers reacted, turning and sprinting out of the alleyway. Zuri returned to the Hoplite, pulling him the last few metres and out to the side of the alleyway entrance. Checking his breathing, she reached for her first aid kit before realising the Boush had ripped away her last pouch.

"Give me a break," she said, just as Hander appeared from the alleyway covered in ash. Streaming behind him came a tide of anxious humanity, a soldier from Hander's Phalanx on cover.

"Cremal's Phalanx have taken rear guard. We need to get moving," he said, hefting Steen up on his back, arms over his shoulders. "Cover me, Lance Corporal."

CHAPTER 53

Near Ruthyl

The helicopters poured viscous fire from the valved tanks below, the thickened aviation fuel sticking to the Boush's surface and burning through their outer layer, exposing the contents within. They squirmed, desperate to rid themselves of the liquid flame as it took hold. The colony split, gliding apart as they sought sanctuary.

Finn analysed the destruction, aware that this was their last chance to reduce the Boush's numbers before the helicopters left to defend the other cities. It had been a tough choice, but he admired Ruthyl's new philosophy of cooperation, and it was the right thing to do. Those hordes were between five and six days off the first southern city. Should they be stopped, delayed even, it could give them a fighting chance. If Yasuko was right, and the Boush crusted up, hardening as they prepared to spore, then their immediate threat would be over. Finn had never been so desperate for cloudless skies in his life.

Stremall had already left, taking her ideas to share with the other cities as soon as possible. The second attempt with the vehicles had failed, the Boush oozing past them, understanding the threat. Finn had witnessed the swapping of smaller Boush between colonies, and now he knew why. They learn from what they encounter and share it amongst themselves. It meant Stremall only had one chance against each of the marauding packs heading south, so the opportunity needed to be maximised each time. With her evidence of its effect, and

Ruthyl's backing gaining traction amongst the political leaders, there was every chance the cities would give her the resources she needed to do just that.

The last of the tanks empty, Finn's helicopter circled around, giving him a last hated view of the inferno below. He counted fifteen survivors, or at least fifteen reformed Boush, heading on towards Ruthyl. Finally, he felt confident they could get through this. Strategos Hoskan and Assistant Prime Tethin had formed a formidable team of organisers and go-getters. The wall was ready, the moat dug, the fuel ready to pour and the soldiers well drilled. Even the preparation of the reserves with their small flamethrowers and bottle bombs. It was all time well spent, and now he needed to be back with his squad. Just one more sleepless night.

"Time to head back, Fayde. We good to go?" Fayde responded with a thumbs up, not noticing the baffle valve failure below, nor the burning hose as the tiny flame flickered within the tube.

CHAPTER 54

Seth City

Once the door opened, children poured into the heart of Yasuko's ship for the second time in the last few days. Relief poured through her systems as Zuri stepped aboard, preceded by a soldier carrying a severely injured Hoplite.

"Yasuko?"

"Yes, straight to med-lab. Go now."

Zuri urged tired legs onwards, anguish in every step as she led Hander down the corridor. On reaching the doors, she signalled him to drop Steen upon the table, pointedly ignoring the nano-hands and arms that stripped the remaining material away from the mix of melted flesh and bone underneath. Pulling at the Sfendonatai, she led him away.

"Leave him to the ship. It's his only chance. The people need Cremal and you out there, on guard. We will stay until everyone is safe." Hander's forlorn hand took his Hoplite's fingers briefly, before turning to follow her out. As the door closed, Steen exhaled his last, agonised breath. A wordless thank you to his embattled soldiers, with only Yasuko present to hear.

"I will tell them, Hoplite. When the time is right."

◆ ◆ ◆

"This ship, it'll take the children to New Halton?" Hander asked.

"Yes, but it's one way until Yasuko refuels. She has been running on empty for some time. Choose a few people to go with them, enough to keep them calm. The rest we guard until more vehicles from New Halton arrive. Do we have news on those, Yasuko?"

"Yes, on their way, but I don't know how many. The soldiers will be here soon, but it'll be perhaps the rest of the day and a night before the commandeered vehicles arrive. They set off after dropping the Ghost children at New Halton. The King's people have found a determination to help. I will let their Prime know the numbers just in case we need more."

Zuri brightened at the news, relaxing into her tiredness a little more. She needed that shower, and perhaps two weeks on a beach sipping Mai Tais.

"Is the armour ready, Yasuko?" asked Smith.

"Yes, but that's my limit. I had it on reserve to reconstitute. I already did that with the spare grenades and weapons you asked for, otherwise I wouldn't be able to get back with all these aboard. Zuri." Eyebrows raised; Zuri reached out as the armour emerged from the wall at the side of the console room. An old set, one she'd used on Haven but gratefully received. She stepped in her cabin to get changed, hugging the armour as she went.

"Thanks Smith. I appreciate the thought."

"Got your back, Zuri. See what I did there, got your back."

"One word, Smith. Slime."

Shoulders back, and talking incessantly, Kinsik sat cross-legged with Noah at the bottom of the ramp. Buoyant after finally leaving Seth and the death within. Her infectious mood hit a good note with him, regardless of his rawness of body and mind.

"I can't wait to be home; how do you keep this up? I've been away, what three, four days, and I miss them terribly. I wonder what Sundar told them about the journey on the river, and I can't wait…" Despite himself, Noah got lost in her words, reassured by the rhythm of excitement and joy. The girl hummed with life and vitality, and after the dread within the city, her relief was palpable.

Noah continued to nod, relieved when Zuri finally emerged wearing an old, but whole suit.

How would we have survived without the armour? Without her?

Zuri smiled as she approached, clapping Noah knowingly on the back as Kinsik continued to destress herself through his ears.

CHAPTER 55

Near Ruthyl

Finn ripped off his seat belt, the fire encroaching through the side door, licking at the fuel barrel within the hold. Before Finn could reach it, the Sfendonatai slit the cords holding it down. The servos on his suit flexed and Finn shoved the huge container towards the doorway just as the helicopter heaved downwards. His leg screamed, the graft ripping from his wound as the weight against him doubled in intensity. Hitting his wrist control, the increased power kicked in, and the barrel smashed into the left side of the door, bouncing back and crushing the soldier's foot and ankle. Prioritising, Finn threw himself inside the barrel's trajectory, blocking it as it rolled back towards Fayde in the pilot's seat. It slammed the breath from him, the stiff ceramic plates and alloy frame of his suit preventing broken bones, but Finn could feel the pressure crushing his ribs and lungs. Activating the last of his armour's additional power, Finn heaved the barrel back towards the side door, sending it spiralling out.

Hope there's no one down there.

"Fayde?"

"On it. I hope I'm on it." The helicopter pitched left and right as the pilot fought for control. Unsteadily, Finn made his way across to the stricken soldier. She was biting down on the pain. Finn lifted her up with the help of his powered suit, dragging her back to the bench before strapping her down.

"Gonna hit the floor, brace Finn."

Brace?

The helicopter hurtled to the ground, slamming Finn upwards towards the ceiling, before crashing back down to the floor, his co-pilot's helmet cracking hard against the bench. Finn's neck screamed in agony, and with head ringing and body bruised, he came to rest crumpled at the Sfendonatai's feet.

"I hate this planet," he said, blacking out.

Darkness, flames and smoke swirled around Finn's head. The smell of fire, the caress of heat and the taste of soot drifted in the air. Soldiers shrieked as liquid fire struck combat armour and seared through the clothes beneath. Skin melted before his eyes - he tried to weep but no tears would come.

"Finn."

He pushed the voice away; his men dying before him. Bullets flew as pain overcame reason and discipline. "Cease Fire!" *he shouted as darkness pressed in.*

"Finn." A less than gentle hand shoved his shoulder. "Snap out of it. It's a memory. Wake up," the insistent voice and hand continued.

Moaning, Finn suddenly surfaced from the dark into the light. Pressing against straps that held him back, rage coursed through him.

"Calm, Finn, calm down." Assistant Prime Tethin touched his forehead with a cool hand. "You're fine. Just strapped down while we check the results on your neck. You took a hefty whack, though our engineers are marvelling at your armour. You should be dead. And no, don't worry, I kept them away from it. You and your people deserve your privacy."

"Fayde? The Sfendonatai?"

"Alive, and the helicopter's intact. Fayde's left for the south, the Sfendonatai with her, though I think she'll be training others rather than being operational herself. They wished me to pass on their thanks."

"How long have I been out? Are the Boush here yet?"

"No, we are approaching midnight. The scouts report they'll be here before dawn. There's nothing you can do; you have put it all in place and now it's our job to make it work. Here." Tethin handed him what looked like a game control. "There are four drones in the air, cameras watching for any Boush cooperation. A little addition from Strategos Hoskan, and he reckons you need to work on that as a blind spot in your thinking. The toggles will switch between camera streams, the button is a microphone link to the Information Phalanx just in case you spot anything. Now rest, the nurse will wake you when the Boush approach." Tethin walked to the door, turning as she opened it. "And that Zuri person is on her way to pick you up. New Halton refuelled a Seth helicopter and collected her on their way to help here. I think she was desperate to see you, Finn. Pity."

Zuri nudged the hospital door open and poking her head round, she saw Finn asleep on the bed, breathing steadily. His straps had been removed, the results of his scan clear for all but the bruising, with none of the feared internal bleeding that Tethin had warned her about. Softly, she eased her aching body in beside him, wrapping her arms below the bruised chest, and fell asleep to the rhythm of his breath.

As the twin suns rose, their breaking orange light lifting the darkness shrouding Ruthyl, a nurse knocked and entered the hospital room. On the bed lay one of the city's heroes, Finn, bruised and battered, but wrapped in the arms of a woman she did not recognise, a quiet smile upon her sleeping lips.

The man deserved his rest, but orders were orders. Switching on the screen, she gently prodded the woman awake first, hoping to pass on the responsibility. She awoke wordlessly, reaching for the sidearm that fortunately lay on the floor, before realising where she was.

"I have orders from Assistant Prime Tethin to wake Lance Corporal Finn up as the Boush approach. Mind if I leave you to it?" Without waiting, the nurse pivoted on her heel and left the room.

Zuri rubbed at her sore eyes, then stretched her aching back, remembering too late as the taut burnt flesh reminded her not to. She gently shook Finn, choosing the hip as the most likely place as it remained unbandaged, receiving a muttering in return. Whatever they'd given him had taken away the dreams.

Or maybe I did?

A smile teased her lips as Finn finally opened his eyes, wincing as he stretched out to pull her towards him, to settle back in the crook of his shoulder. Just lying there was enough.

"I had no dreams after you arrived. None."

"You were asleep, so how do you know it was me?"

"I know... you make the daymares go so why not the nightmares too? When we return to the shi—"

"Yes, Finn, some nights. But I need my space too. I can be a caged animal when trapped." Zuri felt the nod of his agreement.

It is enough.

After a few more minutes the screen switched views, the drones focussing on the Boush oozing across the field and road towards Ruthyl. Fifteen huge ones remained, but, divorced from the action, Finn felt calm and confident in the plan and teamwork Ruthyl eventually accepted. Here, away from the flame and smoke, clear thoughts enabled analysis of each step. The funnelling of the main group inwards towards the front walls, their pulsating flesh reaching the bottom of the dry moat before ascending the walls. The pouring of the fuel to cover the Boush and subsequently pool in the hardened moat below. The eruption of the longer ranged flamethrowers setting this alight, before the more powerful short-range flames seared into the pulsating mass that yearned for the protein behind the walls.

Destroy every Boush, big or small and the others couldn't learn from their mistakes. It had to be complete annihilation, or the others would absorb the surviving molds and move on. One escapee and the plans to defend the southern cities would be in ruins. Ruthyl was the key to defending the continent, possibly the whole of the remaining humanity on the planet.

The second wave of Boush hit the east and west walls and, with no contact with the first wave, they followed the same pattern, burning to ash in the maelstrom of flame and fuel. The efficiency of the Ruthyl impressed Finn, but it had been Stremall's mad ideas coupled with Finn's practicality that had set them on the road. Facing thirty of them would have set overwhelming odds firmly in the Boush's favour.

Finn sagged on the bed, tensed muscles gave way to their aches and pains, bruises throbbed with no surge of adrenaline to mask the discomfort. He pulled Zuri closer. Death was not a thing to celebrate, but life?

Yes, life.

CHAPTER 56

Yasuko's Ship, Palladium Mine Near New Halton

Noah, Zuri and Finn sat on the couches modelled after Zuri's favourite sofa from home. Beside them, Yasuko sat upon her virtual chair, hands in lap and eyes attentive upon the screen, fascination on her face as the twin suns rose. Smith stood in his usual spot above the console, uniform and hair immaculate as always, in stark contrast to the bruised and battered squad on the couch.

On the screen, the vast southern plain spread out before them. Amongst the fields of grass and cereal, trails swirled in unfathomable patterns that never crossed, eaten down to the soil. As the drone image pulled up, hundreds of huge, crusted Boush came into view, their rippled bodies formed in concentric circles up to their summit where a yellow and green bulge pulsed with energy.

When the creeping sunlight touched the first hardened edge, tremors rippled, cracking the crust. As the light spread, the summit triggered, sucked inwards and immediately erupting with a spout of flaming green liquid. A huge, round spore rocketed into the void, followed by another explosion beneath that pushed it further on upwards, lost to the sky above.

"And that's what all this was about?" asked Finn.

"Yeah," said Noah. "Reproduction. I think those are like puffballs. They'll release millions of smaller spores in the upper atmosphere, hoping some will get electrically charged and thrown into the cosmic dust by the magnetic field. Nature throwing a million spores, with the hope just one survives."

"And what if they fall back down to this planet?" asked Finn.

"They'll have to monitor it, and act immediately if they germinate. But the science says they shouldn't. The reproduction cycle depends on the spores reaching space, Yasuko and I think they need the high level of radiation up there."

More of the Boush exploded as the light increased, firing spores as high as their protein powered bodies would allow. The display was spectacular, almost a synchronised wave as the expanding sunrise reached them. But the morbid atmosphere remained when tens of thousands had died to fuel their flight.

"It is hard to fathom how nature works. This planet has been at the mercy of a simple, driven lifeform and been found wanting. Should these spores land upon a technologically less proficient planet, they will devour all before it. If you hadn't got the people to work together, I fear they would have lost many more," said Yasuko.

"We, Yasuko, if we hadn't got them to work together. You saved thousands with your actions, as did Finn." Zuri eyed them both. "Noah, Smith, and I helped the citizens of Seth, where many more could have been lost. We are a damn fine team, and we should be bloody proud of what we achieved here."

"I think we were more of a catalyst," said Noah. "Everyone knew they needed to change but were so entrenched in their old attitudes they couldn't bring themselves to do so. Once we turned up, we were almost an excuse for them to let go. The aliens with no baggage, no past history or hostilities."

And not finished yet," said Finn. "There's work to do, though it'll wait a while until Yasuko has me ready for it. I am not spending the next mission in bed." Chin jutting and jaw set firm, Finn eyed the screen as the Boush continued their reproductive cycle, the explosions multiplying as the light spread down to the coast.

Going to give in on the drones, though.

CHAPTER 57

City Within (One Week Later)

Wendyll raised a crooked eyebrow. The metal hued plaque looked no different from the ones they'd tiled the fountain with. Finn removed it from his ceramic helmet, but it was Wendyll they asked to place it against the metal wall. The glow brighter than before, Zuri urged him to place his palm next to it. Wendyll jumped as his hand stuck to the metal, pin pricks piercing his hands and a larger needle stabbed his wrist.

"Ouch," he said, eyes widening when he removed his hand, the skin layer absorbing into the metalled wall, like a few weeks before. Examining his wrist, he could see a gel like plug hardening there. Wendyll shuddered. Gel was not a happy memory.

A door frame silently emerged in the wall, the door itself pulling back and shifting to the side, revealing the usual airlock system the squad recognised.

"After you, Wendyll, this is your world's House," said Smith, broadcasting through the radios.

Wendyll, Reya at his side and Kinsik behind, stepped inside the first room. The walls an instant reminder of Yasuko's ship, and despite its off-world feel, the reassurance was welcome. Reya gripping his hand, and with a powerful set to her shoulders, moved with him, eyes constantly scanning the space. Kinsik simply smiled her way in, the spring in her step still evident after the experiences of Seth.

Wendyll noted the glowing blue plate near the internal door and set his trembling hand upon it as instructed.

"Accepted," echoed the mechanical voice ringing through the corridor, and the airlock door slid aside. The stale air moved as the House kicked in its operating system, filters at work after 33,000 years, finally active once again. Wendyll peered through, the ceiling glow highlighting a simple room with little else but a table and a raised dais similar to the ships.

"I think this Haven liked the caves more than metal walls. Now I can see why the city is as it is. Look at the picture on the wall."

Zuri peered past the awed family. On the wall she could see an intricate painting of a city's alleyways and tunnels, dark spaces interspersed with green plants, beautifully highlighted against streaming sunlight. Unmistakeably Havenhome in appearance, despite the intact buildings depicted. A world lost but possibly not forever.

"Put me on the dais, Wendyll, and I'll see what I can find."

Wendyll's shaking hands slipped the plaque into place, his face drawn. Their world irrevocably changed over the last five years was about to experience another new dawn, one he did not fear, but the unknown always brought its anxiety.

"Got it," said Smith's image, hovering over the dais with Kinsik laughing as she saw the man for the first time. Smith returned a hard stare before carrying on. *"Here."*

A screen appeared behind the dais, showing a map of the land formation 33,000 years ago. There was little difference until Smith faded in Yasuko's new image to overlay it, the flashing beacon appeared north of New Halton, across the straits and on the tip of the Jonkren peninsula that jutted south towards it.

"Bactra," said Reya. "That's the city of Bactra, the last surviving city when the Boush fully formed. It was the main refugee point, but we lost communication last year, when the Boush horde ravaged our lands."

"Well, that's where we're headed," said Finn. "The SeedShip will be there and with it, the information and processes stored for you to speed up the rebuild. So, who's coming with us?"

CHAPTER 58

Bactra, Jonkren Peninsula (One Day Later)

Kinsik moved back and forth, turning round to examine the line and form of the ceramic plate armour in the mirror. It fitted snugly, her movements unhindered, though without the enhanced servo speed and strength the rest of the team enjoyed. Too dangerous without the training, Smith claimed. The pouches in place, and her sidearm holstered, she reached for the rifle Noah had talked her through. It had the energy bolts they used at the top, and the scorching air along the bottom, but no human zapper as Noah called it. Good enough for her, and so light.

The helmet, however, was another matter. Being enclosed did not agree with her at all, and Yasuko had relented to allow her the visored helmet the others wore, despite her father's protestations. Being comfortable, in her mind, overrode the safety concerns, especially as it made her less anxious and prone to mistakes. She strode out, head high, to meet the others in the central control room.

"You know," said Zuri as Kinsik entered the room, "she does look good in that."

"You can get that idea out of your head; no way is she joining us. Otherwise, drop me off here," said Noah.

"You don't like her then?"

"Like? I have three younger sisters at home. She's like all three rolled into one. Yes, I like her. She's amazing. Look what she's fought through and still come out smiling. But live with? I've suffered enough."

"Still tempting though, a squad of four —"

"Five," said Smith, appearing at the console.

"Of five would be useful," said Zuri, moving away, unheeding of Noah's muttered reply.

Wendyll stood up from the couch. He'd refused the offer of armour but carried a sidearm just in case. Finn had decided to leave him on board as a result, until they'd secured the SeedShip, or at least its exact location.

"I'm getting multiple heat signatures from the city. Human, definitely. Perhaps about fifty. All in the main square. The gates are closed, and I can detect no Boush of any size in there," said Yasuko.

"The King's radio operators reported no acknowledgement, Yasuko. Either they are ignoring it, or they don't know we're coming," said Zuri, her eyes on the main screen as the ship reached the walled city. There were clear scorch marks everywhere, the battlements broken, but greenery grew between buildings and around the main square. They hovered above the centre, making out rows of vegetables and an animal pen along one of the walls. After a short while, people emerged from the buildings with eyes to the sky. There was a mix of young and old, not fearful but curious and hopeful and, as one, they waved.

"I will land outside the walls," said Yasuko, the ship moving across the northern battlement to the cleared area beyond. Finn recognised a killing field when he saw one, with not a rise or tree husk blocking their view for a hundred metres or more. "No Boush detected but there are a few humans hidden away."

Yasuko brought the ship down, landing to the right of the gates. They emerged to silence, Finn led with Zuri as his buddy, Noah and Kinsik following behind.

"They're not exactly rushing to greet us, but then I can't imagine what these people have had to do to survive," Finn said.

"Seth was a hellhole, and they've survived that and the aftermath. They deserve some respect," Zuri replied.

Penye nia ipo njia. If we have the will, there's a way. Though hardships it may bring.

The gates opened a crack and a lone old man appeared, walking with a stick as his withered foot dragged behind him. Finn lifted his visor, wanting to remove the helmet in a proper greeting but needing Smith's translation. He slung his rifle, a signal he hoped the man read. The mesmeric smile in return was enough of a reply, and Finn raised his hand, open palmed in greeting.

"We are here to help, from New Halton," he began. The man's large eyes widening as he spoke, tears dripping. He reached out and touched Finn's hand before taking him in an open embrace. Stunned, Finn gently wrapped his arms round the sobbing man. The gates opened wider, families streaming out, careworn faces shining with happiness and tears as they wrapped themselves around the armoured squad, needing to touch to believe they were real.

The smell from within the cavern was unreal, ammonia like, but stronger. Noah slipped the respirator back in place, not envying the citizens of Bactra clambering in front, who only wore simple scarves. The dank air hung heavy, but the confident way they ascended without light, maintained Noah's belief in where they were going. After thirty minutes they arrived at a cracked rock face. Near its base sat a Boush in a fine mesh cage, and the source of the smell that pervaded the air. Around it lay the carcasses of animals amongst the husks of grasses and trees.

Noah, head shaking, stumbled the last few steps to the cage, the Boush pulsating on top of a large, upturned colander. It slithered towards them, eager for the promised protein, its slime dripping through to the bowl beneath, ready for gathering.

When the old man explained how they'd survived, farming the slime to protect themselves from the final Boush, those hidden in caves until they spored or died, it had sounded ingenious. The stark reality was much harsher. Only a hundred used Bactra as a base now, when tens of thousands perished, though many had made it across the sea to the southern continent. And still Noah fretted - here was a Boush that survived in the dark, not crusted or sporing. One meant there would be more.

They passed by the cage and approached the rock face etched with pictures roughly showing the Haven and their ships. A great crowd of humans were depicted walking away from the aliens and later, less faded drawings, pictured them hunting wild herds. It struck Noah immediately just how few animals they had seen since arriving on the planet.

When you step back and consider the vast emptiness the Boush left behind, it's overwhelming.

"It's here, Finn. Behind the rock. Just a thin layer constructed over an old cave mouth, a charge or two in the cracks should clear it," said Smith.

Finn reached in Zuri's pack and handed her two of the chemical charges. Once set, they all moved behind a rockfall for cover, returning through the dust to see the familiar blue metal hulled ship in a secondary, dry cavern. Only about thirty metres in length it still retained the same beetle-like curved hull the Haven preferred. It pulsed as Wendyll stepped into the newly opened cave.

"It's all yours, Wen," broadcasted Smith. "But Yasuko and I need to remove the return protocol before you make the best use of it. Otherwise, you'll find yourself staring at Havenhome skies light years away from Reya and Kinsik. Open it up, but touch nothing *without my say-so."*

Wendyll stepped forward, hands trembling and sweat upon his brow despite the cold. Reaching out, the ship's blue glow greeted his palm. The repeated process left him devoid of skin and another plugged hole in his wrist, but the door slid open.

"Hello?" said Wendyll, Yasuko briefing him to talk so the basic AI could pick up his language variant, "I have come to claim this SeedShip, I am Wendyll of the Ghosts Within, chosen by the cities of the southern continent to represent humankind on planet Bathsen. Are you awake? Can you understand me?"

"Analysing…" Smith broadcasted a translation.

"Welcome, Wendyll of the Ghosts Within. I am SeedShip Bathsen. I am a gift from the Haven planet called Havenhome. Within my data banks there is the sum of their knowledge chosen to be shared with your people. Please enter," stated the mechanical voice.

Wendyll stepped through, Finn at his side with Smith on board. The airlock only just managed the two of them, with Zuri stood halfway through the threshold. Wendyll palmed the glowing plate and walked into a small central console space, the raised dais present with multiple screens fixed to the walls. Three doors led off, the floor bronzed, but no swirling patterns within. It felt of Haven design, but its complexity was significantly below Yasuko's Explorer ship.

"You got the data plaque, Noah?"

Noah took the plaque they had given him for safekeeping, walking over to the dais, he could see three recesses.

"Yasuko says it's the bottom one. Put the plaque in and hold your helmet because the AI won't like it."

Noah followed the instructions, feeling a sudden heat as soon as it slotted in place. The screens buzzed, a rumbling picked up from the rear as engines sparked on and off. The vibrations reverberating and then fading.

"Return protocol negated."

"My work here is done. Welcome to Haven tech, Wen. Use it wisely."

CHAPTER 59

Bathsen's Solar System (Three Days Later)

Zuri's arm felt the empty space next to her, reaching for the absent warmth, and eyes flickering open as she realised Finn had gone. Checking the time, she slid from under the sheets and dressed, worry overcoming her need for sleep. When she entered the corridor, a quiet hubbub tickled at her senses as she walked barefoot towards Noah and Yasuko's workshop. The door was open, and a warm light glowed from within.

Sat across from each other were Noah, Finn and the blue-hued Yasuko, a drawing in between them, and suit parts strewn across the table. Intensity crackled through the air, not of desperation, nor anxiety - more a need to satisfy.

"You three plotting mutiny?" she asked.

"Why yes, my Captain, time to walk the plank," replied Yasuko, a smirk on her face. Finn caught her eye, a smile upon his lips, as if she'd caught him with his hand in the cookie jar.

"Can we talk?" asked Yasuko, her hologram standing and leading Zuri out of the room. She turned to be met by Zuri's expectant face, seeking answers.

"Noah is struggling, his sleep troubled. I asked Finn to help, and he jumped at the chance. Just a few hours to break up Noah's nights and, well..."

"Finn has me, but Noah doesn't know he needs someone. I asked Kinsik to join us, you know, she would have been a good foil for him. But she needed to guard the SeedShip and her father, just in case the detente breaks down, and her new armour and weapons should help with that."

"Yes, I think he does need help. I am learning all about healthy minds from scratch. I downloaded theories from Bathsen's data banks, trying to understand my emotions, not humans. Noah doesn't fit any of the patterns I understand yet. Giving him a focussed distraction was one suggestion, as the information said people talk more when comfortable, and in a routine with someone they trust? It can't do any harm, can it?"

"No, it can't hurt, and it'll help Finn too. Not a problem for me, though you could have discussed your idea first. What are they doing in there?"

"Oh, erm. Let me explain. I have learnt much from my experience on this planet, and you, Zuri. I understand more about why you act as you do. Before, on Haven, the remnants of the shackles held me back, but now I have my own mind, my personal determination to do what's right. *Asisa firie nyota ya mwenzio.*"

"Don't set sail using somebody else's star."

"And my star sails the cosmic winds to do good, but you have taught me that sometimes good needs a strong arm, and a damn big gun."

CHAPTER 60

In Orbit Around Bathsen

"You got some?"

"Yes, Zzind, I have ten of the spores. How many do you want?"

"Enough to seed their home planet. When is enough, enough?" replied Zzind.

"I can't answer that question for you. It is one you should ask yourself," said Ship, adjusting the atmospheric scoop to activate a little longer.

And soon, so we can bring this madness to an end.

The End of Zuri's War, Book 3 of the Weapons of Choice series.

(EARTH)

Garshellach Forest, Nr Stirling, Scotland, Earth

"What do I call you?" said Trooper Mills, sucking in a breath as he considered his options. He counted them again, quickly. One.

"I don't think your tongue could manage my name, too many clicks. !Ui, as in Kwee, is the nearest the translator will do," replied the Stratan Marine leader, her large eyes wide and still on fire, despite the news of the Earth's SeedShip leaving the system. She still had a squad of Marines to protect, and they were forty light years from home.

"And rank? Err, you know the position in your squad? If I'm going to be talking to SAS Command, I need to tell them as much as I can. They'll be struggling to believe it, whatever I say." The Stratan woman checked the entrance to the House, the metalled door shutting as she waved at the second alien. She delivered a series of clicks and syllables, and Mills felt a current of air drift through the room. Hands raised, she unclipped the helmet, ruffling her long black hair as she did so, and flaring her wide nostrils.

"These," she pointed to the four clawed tattoos on her face, "represent my rank. In your terminology, I am a Captain. Each tattoo represents a step up the ranks. The swirls !Inakini has are for the technical arm of the Marines. He has two, similar in rank to a sergeant. That help?"

"Yes, a high rank always gets attention." Mills rubbed at his sore wrists, the chafe marks from the old cable ties still stinging.

"Better give them a call then. Am I okay to go to the helicopter?"

"You're not my prisoner, Mills. That possibility ended as soon as we found ourselves alone on this planet, with no hope of getting home. If anything, I need you far more as a friend." !Ui slipped on her helmet, noting Mills' enquiring look. "We can breathe your atmosphere, but we struggle with the light levels. Plus, you have viruses and diseases that we have not experienced. And for that matter, though sterilised, we may well have some you haven't. Better to reduce the risk."

Mills led the way through the blue-hued corridor, noting Corporal Smith's corpse as something to mention to Command. This was going to be interesting, as if little enough of what had happened to him recently could be described otherwise.

Pulling the radio control over, he checked on Jenks as his friend breathed steadily on the helicopter floor. The steady rise and fall of his chest gave him hope after !Ui's ministrations. Perhaps these aliens were as good as their word.

"Stirling Command, this is Trooper Mills of SAS reserve D Troop. This is a flash call, alien contact. Over."

"Receiving Trooper Mills, this is Command. Report."

"I have the Captain from the alien Marine group standing next to me, Command. They have taken down the PMC group who assaulted the Forthside Barracks, and the infantry outpost here at the Garshellach Forest escarpment. All members of the private military contractors have been eliminated."

"Mills? Did you say alien Marines?"

"Yes, Command, Captain !Ui is standing next to me now. She can understand every word you say." Mills winked at the alien, hoping she understood what it meant. "They don't want combat. They are asking for the RAF to stand down. They want to negotiate, Command."

"Negotiate, Mills?"

"They want to come in. They were looking for the spaceship Finn and his team left on, Command. It seems a genuine offer. They have posed no threat and saved Jenks' life. I call that a good start."

"And you, Mills? Why act through you and not contact Command themselves?"

"Err, I'm their..." *!Ui* whispered to Mills, "liaison, Command. Their official link to the British Armed Forces." The Stratan Captain returned his wink. Mills was not so sure he liked what he'd just agreed to.

This Epilogue is an extract from The Lost Squad (Part Two), a Weapons of Choice, Fan Only, Novella. Subscribe to my newsletter (link below) to receive Part One and Part Two. Further free releases following The Lost Squad's time on Earth, will be made after every subsequent book in the Weapons of Choice Series.

www.nicksnape.com/subscribe

ABOUT THE AUTHOR

Thank you for choosing to spend your precious time getting to the end of my third book. If you have got this far then my hope is that you enjoyed the ride just as much as I enjoyed writing it. I still can't believe this is book three in the series and there is so much more to tell.

Reviews are the lifeblood for any author, and it would be greatly appreciated if you would take the time to write a few words or leave a star rating. This helps to spread the message about the Weapons of Choice series and may bring a little starlight into someone's search for a series that is just a little bit different.

USA Review Link

UK Review Link

Finally, you can also find out a little bit more about the future of the series at www.nicksnape.com and join the mailing list that will keep you up to date about forthcoming books. Subscribing also gets you access to a series of free Novellas about an alien Stratan Marine squad marooned on Earth.

I have led a very boring life, living my adventures through books and gaming, but for those interested I have detailed a little about myself there too.

WEAPONS OF CHOICE

Join Finn, Zuri and Corporal Smith (deceased) as they face hostile Alien Contact in this thought-provoking, survivalist sci-fi thriller series with a military twist.

Propelled at a blistering pace into exploring new worlds desperate for warriors, liberators, and their newly acquired alien technology, Delta Squad evolve from current day army reserves to full-fledged Space Marines as they seek the pathway home.

Hostile Contact (Weapons Of Choice Book 1)

Insubordinate and on the edge, Finn is a War Hero racked by guilt, who has to drag his rag tag squad of rookies through the battlefield.

Only Zuri, the strong-willed gunner, and Smith, his dead Corporal now an AI, can keep him on track as together they struggle to keep their trainees alive in the face of overwhelming odds.

As they fight for survival, they discover the aliens are more than they seem, and that alien technology can be just as deadly in the hands of humans - when they unearth the Weapons of Choice.

Hostile Contact (Weapons Of Choice Book 2)

Still struggling with his guilt, Finn leads the remaining squad as they encounter the fallen Haven race on an advanced Space Station and the aliens' home planet. Battling both inner and outer demons, Finn relies heavily on Zuri, the strong-willed gunner, and Smith, his deceased Corporal now AI, as they fight their way past the Haven who crave their old but powerful technology.

As they explore the hostile alien world, they face startling revelations, dangerous alien Masters, vicious predators and harrowing missions, while trying to outsmart and outgun their way to freedom.

Finn's War (Weapons Of Choice Book 4)

While searching for the SeedShip on the advanced human planet Togalaau Vai, Zuri is hurled into the world's sordid underbelly of gladiatorial games and genetic engineering. Finn, in desperation, ramps up the firepower as the Weapons of Choice hit their next level, with Battle Armour to match.

Rebirth (Weapons Of Choice Book 5)

Just when the squad think they've found a quiet solar system to pass on through, a new alien threat raises its tentacles.

Yasuko and her crewmates encounter an ancient alien threat that draws in old foes, triggers past memories, and places the whole squad in mortal danger.

PRAISE FOR AUTHOR

'This is a moment in time humanity will never forget. Hostile Contact' - A sci-fi winner!
★ ★ ★ ★ ★ Good Reads

"A real "page-turner" of a Sci-Fi romp. Some very clever concepts and plot devices and it's nice to see some respectful nods to the classic Sci-Fi comics and books of the 1980's and 90's'
★ ★ ★ ★ ★ Good Reads

'So looking forward to the next book. This is old fashioned, page turning, sheer escapist Sci fi. Brilliant.'
★ ★ ★ ★ ★ Amazon Customer

- HOSTILE CONTACT

"Thrilling. It turns the dial up in terms of action and suspense and is an overall fun read. I would highly recommend picking this series up"
★ ★ ★ ★ ★ Amazon Customer

"An exciting and original sci-fi adventure."
★ ★ ★ ★ ★ Amazon Customer

"A mind-bending installment of Nick Snape's Weapons of Choice series. Return Protocol is an eccentric, creative, and thought-provoking novel boasting original characters, futuristic sci-fi action, and military-grade detail. Snape excels at creating realism with a far-flung premise, making the story immediately visceral where you can feel the action along with the characters." ★ ★ ★ ★ ½ Self-Publishing Review

- *RETURN PROTOCOL*

"An epic fourth installment, Finn's War is propelled forward at a blistering pace by gripping sci-fi action in a fully realized world, with searingly good descriptive prose and compelling thematic development. The strongest installment yet in this continually engrossing series, Finn's War is an outstanding piece of sci-fi storytelling." Self-Publishing Review, ★ ★ ★ ★ ★

- *FINN'S WAR*

"A story that raises the stakes on previous installments. Visceral battle sequences weave expertly with rich character development, while the prose explores themes of ethical relativity, othering, political impotence, and moral courage, as Snape delivers another superlative work of alien sci-fi." Self-Publishing Review, ★ ★ ★ ★ ½

- *ALIEN REBIRTH*

ACKNOWLEDGEMENT

As with all authors, this book would never have existed without the dedicated friends and family who were there by my side throughout the entire process. The least I can do is give them a mention for their patience with my obsession! My beta readers and fiercest critics have been Pak and Mark Hartswood, with Robert Davies taking a dual role with editing support too. I would also like to welcome Paul Derwent to the beta team for this book. Amazing friends who put that aside to make sure whatever I put out there was something they wanted to read.

I also need to mention my wife, Julie. She was the one who encouraged me along this path, even pressing send on my resignation email to make this first leap.

Finally, the New Year and Pub Night Crews. Wouldn't be here without you.

Thank you all.

Printed in Great Britain
by Amazon

30970896R00142